With a
Vengeance

Gerald DiPego

WITH A VENGEANCE

McGraw-Hill Book Company

NEW YORK   ST. LOUIS   SAN FRANCISCO   DÜSSELDORF
MEXICO   PANAMA   TORONTO

The persons and events in this book are entirely fictitious.
Any resemblance to those living or dead is purely coincidental.

Book design by Lynn Braswell.

123456789BPBP7987

LIBRARY OF CONGRESS CATALOGING IN PUBLICATION DATA

DiPego, Gerald.
With a vengeance.
I. Title.
PZ4.D596Wi   [PS3554.I63]   813'.5'4   76-30472
ISBN 0-07-017012-6

To Pauline,
who always knew

THE DREAM

SOME *large, weaving, brush-breaking thing was moving through the forest, shouting and laughing in many voices, its mouths puffing steam into the chilled night. It stumbled into a clearing lighted by a campfire and became five young men, one tied and blindfolded and carried by the others.*

They dropped Randal Nye and walked to the campfire where another man was waiting, tending the flames—five men around the fire like thumb and fingers curled about the palm of a hand, and for one part of a second they were still, caught between words, between motions, between this moment and the rest of their lives.

William Davis, the tallest, stood with his hands in the pockets of his short jacket, his elbows thrust out like great wings. His head was lowered, and he seemed about to flap his arms and float upward with the disappearing smoke.

Edward Johns was weak with silent laughter. He was bent forward, his hands on his knees, his mouth gaping as if with a scream.

Dan King stood on one foot, holding the other out high, close to the fire, looking like a nimble dancer in a kick line.

Ben Groff was thrusting a long branch into the heart of the fire. It lighted and, for that moment, connected him with the flames.

Frank Skate had closed his eyes against the stinging smoke, and he stood like a sleeper in their midst, with his palms pushed forward, trancelike.

Five faces in the firelight, young faces, the oldest, twenty-two, the youngest, twenty.

The moment of stillness dissolved in random motions and words. The fire crackled loudly. Randal Nye shouted to be free. They turned to him and began to make the sounds of wolves, of bears and lions. Randal laughed, then cursed them. They went to him and sat him against a tree.

William Davis pulled down his blindfold, left it around his neck like a bandana.

Edward Johns and Dan King untied him and brought his arms back around the tree.

Ben Groff went back to the fire and fed it branches and twigs, built it to a blaze.

Frank Skate pulled something from his pocket that sparked silver in the firelight—handcuffs. He put them on Randal's wrists, locked them.

"See you in the morning, Nye."

"No. Hey! Wait!"

"If the wolves don't get you."

"The bears."

"Lions."

"Mosquitoes!"

"The dark."

Their voices mingled into a single sound as they walked out of the firelight and became one large hulking thing again, cracking twigs and leaves as it moved away through the forest.

Randal Nye was alone, trapped against a tree and not yet afraid. The small animals skittering in the brush did not startle him. The dark treetops, their black branches reaching for him like claws, did not threaten him. He sat and chuckled over the joke that was being played on him, and already in his mind he was telling his friends about it, telling his mother, his father. It was later when his fear began. It was because of the fire.

"Hey! Hey, can you guys still hear me?"

There were no other voices in the forest.

"Can anybody hear me!"

There was no sound but the fire.

"The fire is spreading! Hey! Jesus! PLEASE!"

The campfire had been too large, too hot. A dead bush had ignited near by. The flames had spread. The fire was making a circle around the clearing, igniting the next bush, the next tree, waiting then jumping, jumping toward Randal Nye.

He screamed, and there were no longer any words in his scream, just a deep, mindless sound. His body was a frenzy of kicking and twisting. His wrists began to bleed.

He sucked in burning air and screamed again—and was answered. Someone else was there, rushing toward the clearing, thrusting his hands toward the fire, toward Randal Nye. In one hand he held, between finger and thumb, the key to the handcuffs. He pushed this hand ahead of him, through the flames, through the waves of heat, through the screams. He pushed the key toward the tiny lock on the handcuffs, stretching forward until his bones became fluid, his limbs rubber. His right arm was impossibly long and still stretching longer, but not long enough to reach the lock on the cuffs on the bloody wrists.

Randal Nye screamed a last scream as the thin pine tree caught fire and took him into its flames.

Stephen Nye always awakened at that moment of the dream. He awoke now and sat up, sweating, his heart attacking his chest with quick, powerful blows. He held his trembling hands out in front of him. He thrust his right hand forward and closed his eyes. Once awake, he would always give the dream a different ending. He would always feel the key slip into the lock. He would turn the key and feel the cuffs fall away. He would take his son into his arms and run, carrying his boy into the cold, still forest, both of them weeping.

Then Stephen Nye would weep, sitting there in his bed, weep for Randal, dead twenty years.

1

STEPHEN Nye's body made no statement. It wondered. It asked. His slight curve of back and stoop of shoulder apologized for his height and made of him a question mark. His body never said, "I am passing," but only, "May I pass? May I stand here? May I sit a while?" A weak smile asked forgiveness for his handsome face, blunted that face and made it easy to forget. His eyes said, "Don't worry. I threaten no one." His eyes made him nearly invisible.

"Any questions about this?"

Of the thirty-six students, only two looked at Nye, looked and looked away. Most of the faces were dead, the eyes dull and drifting.

"What about the ending?"

Two girls began talking to each other. It was loud. It was rude. Nye ignored them.

"Were you surprised? Don't all answer at once."

That last part, that small joke, was swallowed. Nye had a good, rich voice, and he used it to give information, to say what needed to be said. If he thought of something extra, a comment, a joke, a curse, a laugh, his voice changed, dropped, sent the words out in a weak lob to fall at the listener's feet. No one heard.

"Sort of surprising," a student said.

"Sad," said another.

Then there was silence but for the two talking girls.

Nye smiled at them. "Girls." He swallowed that one and had to do it again. "Girls. Please."

They hardly acknowledged him. They stopped for a moment, not at all embarrassed, still glancing at each other. Soon they were whispering again.

"What do you mean, 'sad,' John? Why is it sad?"

"Well, he's alone now, and his father's dead—shot by DeSpain. The boy is just . . . walking into the woods. He's just . . ."

The student faltered, and the space between his words was filled by the whispering of the two girls. Nye seemed not to hear them. His eyes avoided them, but his mind attacked. His imagination sent out a large hand at the end of an impossibly long arm. This hand spread over the face of one of the girls and closed, crunched her head into a baseball, snapped it from her neck and tossed it through the window with a great cymbals crash of breaking glass. His long, rubbery arm twitched, and the hand now lunged at the second girl, the fingers pushing deep into her stomach and through her stomach to her spine. Nye broke her backbone between two fingers, and she slid to the floor like a sheet of paper. All of this happened in one instant, all within the pause between the student's "He's just . . ." and Nye's, "Yes, go ahead."

"He's just running away from his whole life."

Nye nodded, pacing slowly to the other side of the room. The girls were still whispering, but he didn't hear them. He had destroyed them for today, canceled them from his mind with the same rubbery cartoon violence he had been using to destroy his enemies for sixty-three years.

"What's he really running from," Nye asked them. "And where is he heading?"

During his free hour, Nye walked across the campus, into the park. He could walk for miles, usually at a quick march, in cadence with his thoughts, and if those thoughts trailed back twenty years to that forest, to that phone call, to that funeral, then he would be almost running, whipped and driven by memories still so clean and sharp-edged.

His walk was almost leisurely now, slowing as he neared the park. The images in his mind were bright, soothing pictures, for he was back thirty-five years, and Randal was four, and the two of them were walking together in this very same park.

"Daddy. Look. Look, Dad. Da-ad. Look." Stephen

turned, and Randy was walking on his knees, pitching forward now and landing face down in the grass. He lay still.

"Are you all right?"

The boy didn't move.

"What are you doing?"

"Shh."

"Randy?"

"I'm listening."

"To what?"

"The ground."

"What's it saying?"

"Ouch. Ouch. Ouch."

"Ouch?"

"Every time somebody walks on it."

Stephen's face wrinkled and bunched, uncovering his teeth, hiding his eyes, introducing a small, silly laugh, much higher than anyone would expect. It was a child's laugh.

Randy looked at him, suddenly alarmed. "Just think of all the ouches it's saying right now. Just think of people *digging!*"

Nye smiled and waved the boy forward, took a step. "Come on."

"Dad, you stepped right on it!"

"Can't help it. Sorry, ground. Now come on."

"I don't want to hurt it."

"What're you going to do? Fly?"

The boy rose to his knees and stared at his father, very serious. "Carry me."

Nye lost his smile and went to Randy, picked him up and held him close, carried him home so his tiny shoes would not bruise the ground.

Nye sat on a bench near the empty playground. At sixty-three he looked fifty. His age was in and under and behind his eyes, eyes brimming with memories now.

"Dad, push me."

"You can pump yourself, Rand."

"One push."

"Okay, one."

He actually rose from the bench and walked to that empty swing, touched it. He felt a bit foolish. There were other people in the park, maybe watching the tall old man in the playground. He felt like going home. He could walk home and call up and say he was ill. Someone else could take his classes. He had never done that before. He had always worked when he was able. Maybe it was time to stop. Time to begin.

He glanced at the street he would follow home. He owned no car. Soon after Randal's death came the divorce, and he had gladly given his wife the car. She had gladly taken it and driven out of Iverson and away from a man who brooded and wept and seldom spoke and never laughed his small, high laugh. "Nothing motivates you now," she had said. "You have no motives left, no goals. Why live?" She was wrong. He had already decided. He was already waiting. Perhaps it was time to start.

He had decided at the funeral, looking at the faces of the five young men. The entire fraternity had come, forty-seven bowed heads, a few tears, and in front, the five of them, standing there guilty, ashamed, sorry, suffering. Stephen had stared at them, stared at their faces, their hands, their clothes. He heard the minister speak the word *fate*. He had heard it often then. "Fated to happen." "It was his fate." "The boy's fate was to bless this world for nineteen years and then expire in a cruel accident. . . ." *Fate* and *accident* in the same sentence. But Stephen was not confused. He accepted what was told him. "Those five men . . . they were Randal's fate." But he added to that. Inside his mind, he spoke the words, "Yes, and I am theirs."

He felt the canvas seat of the swing, imagined Randy in it, the back of his head, small shoulders, little legs dangling.

"One underpush, Daddy. Please. Okay?"

Nye curled his fingers into the canvas straps and pulled the swing up against his chest.

"A good one. Okay?"

He smelled the boy's hair, a scent thirty-four years old, kept safe and fresh in his mind, along with a certain pair of short pants and red sneakers and a doll-like sweatshirt and other memories folded neatly and stored within reach.

"Come on, Dad."

The tall, old man ran in the empty playground, holding the empty swing, pushing it, ducking under it and running through the sand. He stopped and turned and watched the boy disappear, heard the flutelike laughter dissolve, stared at the swing until it stopped and hung there, still.

He didn't care if anyone was watching him. He didn't care if they could tell he was crying. It didn't matter anymore. He was finished with them all. He had begun something new.

He didn't go home. He walked to his classroom. He

was late. The students stared at him, and he stared back without apology. In his mind he was punching them goodbye, sending thirty fists out across the room to plunge into those faces. The faces were made of rubber, and his hand went through and stretched out the backs of their heads. He felt the tight rubber on his right hand. "Goodbye," he said, but they didn't hear him. They turned to each other in wonder as he walked out the door.

He went to the office of Everett West, the President of Iverson Junior College.

"He's on the phone."

"I'll wait." His smile said, That's all right. Don't mind me. I'll just sit here. No hurry. The secretary barely looked up from her typing.

She was sedate and correct, fingers curled above the keys, white blouse ironed smooth, smooth young face unbroken by his presence. There were secrets, though, only half-hidden, hints of passion in the loose lock of hair that romped down her forehead and the unbuttoned middle button of her crisp blouse.

Nye saw the light on her telephone wink out. He didn't want to seem pushy, to tell her her job. She glanced at the phone but kept typing. She knew West had finished his call. Nye thought perhaps she had forgotten him. He coughed, moved in his chair, shuffled a foot on the floor. She stopped typing, pulled the paper out of the machine and began to read it. Nye went for her throat.

He reached out with fingers long as ropes for the white flesh above her white collar, but that imaginary hand took over, moved by itself, missed the throat and went for the neck of her blouse, grabbed cloth and pulled hard. The blouse was torn to her waist. She kept reading. He stared at her, surprised at what his mind had done to her, at the sight of her large breasts supported in a loose, lacy bra. He hooked a finger into the center of the bra and yanked it off, straps and all. Her breasts jiggled with the force of it, but still she concentrated on the letter she had typed, correcting an error now with white liquid and a tiny brush, leaning over so that the soft brown skin around her nipples touched the desk top.

Nye wanted her now, as he had not wanted a woman in years, or maybe never before. His cartoons of violence had never been so full of lust. He felt a tingling and thickening between his legs. His mouth was dry. She was leaning over, dabbing with that tiny brush.

He sent out his boneless, fluid arms to stretch across the room and take her. His hands closed on her breasts and pulled. Now she noticed him. She screamed. He pulled her over the desk top, scattering papers, spilling the little bottle of white liquid. He pulled her toward him by her breasts, stretching that tender flesh closer and closer to him as she toppled off the desk, as he dragged her along the floor. She was screaming for help, her breasts yards long now, close to his face. He was trembling. His erection was hard and full. He opened his mouth and closed his teeth on one of the nipples. She wailed. He chewed, and the nipple squeaked like rubber.

Everett West suddenly opened his office door, and Stephen jumped, stiffened in his chair, blinking away the image he had made.

"Hi, Stephen."

The secretary looked up from her letter. "Oh yes. You were on the phone so . . ."

"Well, I hope I didn't keep you waiting long."

"No." Nye's smile was a bit shaky. He waited for his erection to recede.

"What can I do you for, Stephen?"

"Well . . ." He slowly rose. He was much taller than West. He tried to gather his thoughts, quiet his heart. The secretary was typing again. "Ev . . . I just . . . I have to leave now."

West was puzzled. "Oh? You're not feeling well?"

"I mean . . . leave my job."

"I don't understand."

"I'm retiring."

West stared a moment, lost his friendliness. "Now?" Stephen nodded. West stretched a grin over his anger. "Come into my office."

"I really have to quit, Ev."

"But it's—"

"I know. Middle of the term. I'm sorry. Can't . . . go on with it. It's time."

Take some time off, Stephen. A week if you like."

"It's time, Ev. I'm sorry."

"Are you ill?"

"I can't go on with it."

West unmasked his anger, stared Stephen down, made him look at the floor. "At least give me a few weeks to replace you."

"I wish I could, Ev."

"Have you seen a doctor? I mean, if a doctor says you have to, then you have to. But otherwise it's not fair to the school."

"I've taught here thirty-seven years."

"I'm aware of that. I'm aware of that, Stephen. But to stop in the middle of the term."

"I'm really sorry, Ev."

"Think about it. Go home and give it some thought."

"No, I'll just . . . go to my office now and get a few things. I'm finished." He turned and went to the door, feeling West's eyes digging into his back, trying to hurt him. They couldn't hurt him. He was finished with all of them now.

He went to his office, unlocked the door and entered the tiny room, his movements made efficient and unconscious by years of repetition. The desk chair creaked beneath him in the same old key, and his right hand dropped automatically to the level of the file drawer, pulled it out.

Among the folders were five which bore the names of the men who had killed Randal. These folders contained some newspaper clippings and photos, but mainly the notes he'd made as he kept each file up to date. Four of them contained letters, for all but one of the young men had, in time, put his sorrow and shame into words. All the letters had come within a month of the funeral.

Stephen pulled out the folders, but he didn't open them. He only stared at the names.

DAVIS, WILLIAM N.
40
Married (Janice)
C.P.A. Partnership
Davis and Ralph

1312 Hoyt Ave.
Hammond, Ind.

   2 Children
   Robert, 19—University of
              Wisconsin
   Diane, 16

GROFF, BENJAMIN L.
41
Married (2nd Wife) Alberta
Community Relations Exec.
Crescent Park Hospital
New York City

   1 Child
   Donald, 12

JOHNS, EDWARD
42
Married (Irene)
Teacher/Coach
Fairburn H.S.
Fairburn, Ohio

   3 Children
   Thomas, 18—University of
              Missouri/Columbia
   Jason, 16
   Estelle, 12

KING, DANIEL T.
41
Married (2nd Wife) Claire
V.P./Sales Representative
Cal-Vy Sporting Equipment
1113 Wabash Blvd.
Chicago, Illinois

SKATE, FRANK N.
42
Divorced
Occupation?
23 Ashton Place
San Francisco, Calif.

    1 Child
    Ellen, 18

2

DRIVING, in hot, overbright Los Angeles, Ellen Skate searched through her mind the way she would look through her purse, pulling things out, examining them, stuffing them back in. Something important was coming, scheduled, certain. But she couldn't find it, couldn't fill in the blank.

She parked her Volkswagen, turned the key, opened the door and stepped out in one easy flow of motion, crossing the street through a break in the traffic. When she moved, her long hair followed her, floating just behind, never seeming to catch her because Ellen was always moving on from where she had just been, running, driving, sitting on the edges of chairs, tossing her head as she talked, as she laughed. She was small, just over five feet, trim and tan in jeans and a white Mexican shirt, bounding up an outside staircase now, moving toward the door on the first landing, her dark hair following like a flag.

She knocked loudly. "Peter?"

No answer.

"I know you're in there and I want my cassette player and my cassettes not only because they're mine but because you don't deserve them!"

No answer.

"At the count of three I'm going to start shouting all your secrets to the neighborhood beginning with how you can't sleep unless . . ."

Peter's friend, Willy, opened the door. She brushed past him. "Hi, isn't he here? I want my cassette player." She was walking into the bedroom. "I bring my music into this place . . . that's very personal, someone's favorite music. I bring it; I play it and share it. *My* music fills *his* room, even when I'm not there. I leave some of myself to sing to him—and he tries to rip me off."

Willy stood in the bedroom doorway, watching her search the place. He was a muscular young man with a large sensitive face and wire-frame glasses.

"It's under his bed."

"Thanks, Will." She pulled it out, then reached deep under the bed and swept an arm along the floor, gathering tape cassettes, clumps of dust, and a dirty sock. She rose and turned on the tape player. "It better work." She let it play a moment, sitting on the bed and looking up now at Willy. She snapped off the music. "He told me it wasn't here. Can you imagine?" Willy walked toward her, lumbering a bit. "He was just mad." He got on hands and knees and did a slow push-up, lowering his body to look under the bed. He came up with one more dusty cassette, handed it to her.

"Thanks." She was making a stack of cassettes on the bed, growing thoughtful. Willy sat next to her, his weight spilling the stack. He started building it again, his big, blunt fingers carefully balancing the plastic boxes.

Ellen watched him, realizing she felt closer to Willy than to Peter. She had laughed and danced and made love with Peter, but with Willy she had stayed up all night talking, and she had gone on long walks with him where neither of them said a word. She could almost call Willy a friend, almost wrestle with Willy in the grass. That was her image of friendship. If someone was a real friend, you could tackle him, and the two of you could wrestle on the soft grass, rolling and laughing, pinning and being pinned, grabbing and pulling and never hurting.

But then Willy said, "You want to make it, Ellen?" He said it with his eyes on the cassettes, with his fingers carefully building a tower of cassettes.

She stared at him, surprised, hoping he was kidding. He lay back on the bed, slowly, with great muscle control, landing so softly he didn't even topple the tower. One thick hand gently gripped his wire glasses, took them off. He turned to her, smiling. "Why don't we do it?" he said.

Ellen stared a moment more. Then she stood up, and the cassettes fell, and she was snatching them off the bed. "Jesus, Willy."

"Why not, El?"

"Jesus!"

She turned to the door, hunched over with an armful of cassettes, carrying the player. She froze. Peter was in the doorway, looking at her disgustedly, and Willy was saying, "See? See, Pete, I told you."

She knew what Peter was going to say, and she was throwing the cassette player at him even as he said it."

"I bet him you'd say yes," Peter said, and the cassette player hit him in the chest. "Son of a *bitch!*"

She was past him already, screaming toward the door. "You're so *ugly* inside! Your mind is *ugly*, Peter, you goddamn . . ." She was dropping cassettes and Peter was rushing after her, snatching them up off the floor, thrusting the player at her.

"Here. Here! Take your stuff! . . ." He caught her and turned her, spilling the cassettes, pushing the player at her. "Here!"

Peter's face was just inches away, turning red, neck stretched, lips twisted, but it was Willy she was staring at. He stood in the bedroom doorway, smiling. She would never wrestle with him, laughing, two sweating grass-stained pals. Never.

"I hate you!"

"Out! Bitch!"

Peter was pushing her out the door. She swung at him and hit the door frame, didn't notice the pain. He tossed some cassettes after her and she let them fall, then kicked them off the stair landing. The door was banged shut and locked and she turned to it, screaming.

"You two are nothing! You're big blanks! White space!"

She trotted down a few stairs, stopped and shouted to the neighborhood. "Peter can't fall asleep unless somebody holds his feet!"

She arrived at her apartment more sad than angry, thinking of Willy. Her roommate, Ann, yelled from the shower.

"Who's there?"

"A rapist."

Ellen stretched out on the couch and closed her eyes. She liked Ann, but she would never tackle her. If she knocked Ann down on the grass and pinned her, Ann would stare, surprised, wondering. Ellen had seen that stare, that look that said, "My God, what are you dong?" It made her shrink inside.

She sat up, picked up the phone and dialed her mother in San Diego. Her father spent most of his time in an apartment in L.A. Ellen had been on her own for a year. She was taking a few courses at UCLA, studying dance, going to movies.

Busy line.

"Who're you calling?" Ann ambled in, drying her hair.

"My mom. I think I might go down there for the weekend. Two ladies-of-the-beach, burning together on the sand."

"You see Peter?"

"No." She was dialing again. This time it rang.

"Hi, it's me."

Ellen put her feet on the coffee table, and sank deep into the couch. Ann left the room. Ellen's mother said, "Oh," in her mildly surprised way.

"Have you been talking about me?" Ellen said.

"What do you mean?"

"Just a feeling I've got today. Something's going to happen. Maybe Dad's planning something."

"Your father only plans things for himself."

"Well, anyway, I'm having quite a day. Do you think you could stand a visitor?"

"What?"

"What if I come down for the weekend?"

"When?"

"The weekend. Saturday and Sunday is the weekend, Mom."

"This coming?"

"Yes."

"Oh."

"I'll stay at the beach most of the time. I just need . . ."

"You just need someplace to sleep. I know."

"Mom, I'd *like* to spend some time with you. I just *mean* you don't have to stay home if you have plans."

"I may have a guest. I don't know yet."

"Oh. Okay then."

"Maybe next weekend, Ellie."

"Yes. Sure. I have to go now. Bye."

She hung up, got off the couch, and took a few mindless steps around the room. She put her hands in her back pockets and started swaying her hips to some music in her mind.

"Something is going to hap-pen," she said in time to

the music. Her eyes were sad. "Something is go-ing to hap-pen."

Ann shouted from her room. "What?"

"Yeah," Ellen said to herself. "What."

3

I T WAS just after dark on the eve of his new life, and Nye was drinking to that. He sat back and put his feet up and sipped a second glass of burgundy, resting from the great ransacking of his house.

This was the night for packing, and Stephen was traveling light. This was the night for shaking the past out of its hiding places and examining all of its pieces, selecting a few, discarding many. Every drawer pulled out, every closet door opened had unleashed a dozen memories. A hundred Randy Nyes ages two to nineteen years, rushed about the house. Stephen's wife, Elaine, was sitting before him on the floor, a recent bride, and she was poised at the front door, middle-aged and about to leave him forever. She was also taking a shower, and when the water stopped and she emerged, she might be pregnant with Randy or maybe a new mother with large nursing breasts or forty years old and wearing the same face as the image that stood at the door, about to leave him forever.

He stood up and walked amid the rubble—cardboard boxes, stacks of papers, photos and files, suitcases and trunks, drawers stacked like steps against the wall. He surveyed, selected, grabbed a handful of folders, themes written by students, the useless thoughts of strangers writing about the works of other strangers. He threw them all into one of the large plastic leaf bags he had opened in the center of the living room. He had spent hours reading and judging and grading those themes. He was throwing his past away by the handfuls, hours and days of it at a time. He would save only a few moments.

He finished his wine and dropped the glass, too, into the plastic bag. He put his hands on his hips and looked around again, his eyes challenging every piece of the rubble—are *you* important? You? Do I need *you*? Do I take *you* with me?

He stepped over things and walked through the ideas, the memories and visions. It was strange to feel crowded in this house which had seemed so empty for so long. There had been only his step on the floors, only his voice in the rooms, his presence. Now Randys and Elaines hurried about, laughing, shouting, whispering, crying.

"Daddy, can you fix . . ."

"Stephen, did you remember . . ."

"Dad, where's the . . ."

"Steve, are you ready?"

"Daddy?"

Everywhere he looked, a child played or a teen-ager looked up, smiled, a young man flopped into a chair. "Hi, Dad, have you eaten?"

Elaine brushed by him, just out of the shower, water still beaded on her legs beneath the short robe. She turned to him and smiled shyly as she walked into the bedroom, her shyness enticing him to follow. She looked about twenty-five, he thought, when her hair had been . . . . "Stephen, can you give me a hand?" an older Elaine called to him from the kitchen. A younger one was just coming through the door, carrying grocery bags. "Help! They're slipping!"

He went to the burgundy, thought about retrieving his wine glass from the bag, then sipped from the bottle. He wouldn't have dinner tonight—just the wine, and for company he'd have the ghosts. They were jangling his nerves, especially the Stephens, the visions of himself.

He was coming through the front door, grinning, about thirty years younger, lots of brown hair on his head. "Hello!" Old Stephen sat on the couch, crushing papers and file folders, sipping wine and watching his thirty-year-old ghost. Young Stephen was greeted by a young Elaine and a Randy of nine or ten. "I've got something to show you two." He put his briefcase down, unbuttoned his suit coat. "You ready? Better sit down."

Elaine sat on the couch near the old Stephen, who was silent, watching. Randy sat on the floor. Young Stephen went on. "I was giving a great lecture today. American Lit., really had their attention, but I noticed they were focused on my chest. My chest! Look." He opened his suit coat, showing a large, round ink stain on the breast pocket of his shirt. "Look at that! I had my pen clipped in there without the top on it!" Elaine smiled. Randy giggled. Even old Stephen grinned a little at the comedian with all that brown hair. "Look. It goes through!" He was unbuttoning his shirt, showing them the stain on his undershirt, on his skin. Elaine was laughing now and so was Randy. The boy sat cross-legged on the floor, hands on his knees, rocking and giggling.

Old Stephen stood up, blinked away the ghost of Elaine and the ghost of himself. He left Randy there on the floor, rocking, giggling. He walked close to the boy, stared at him, at the little hands gripping the knees, at the eyes alight with laughter. He walked around the boy, listening to that laugh, holding himself back from trying to reach down to the ghost, pick him up, hug him, feel the laughter shaking the little body as he hugged him.

Stephen blinked away the image of Randy. He stood in the silent living room a moment, then walked to his bedroom, seeking a different ghost. He looked inside and watched Elaine take off that short robe, her hair wet from the shower, body shining. She saw him and blushed, and he wanted to lunge through the years, touch that cool, wet flesh, press that shy girl against him. But Randy was calling him back into the living room with the voice of a young man, "Dad, can we talk now?"

He left Elaine. Randy was sitting on the edge of the couch, concerned. "Can we talk about it, Dad? I want you to feel better about it."

"It's your decision, Rand." He said that aloud—old Stephen did—shocked at the sound of his voice. The ghost answered him.

"Sure, but I want you to feel *good* about it. They're nice guys, Dad. They'll be good friends. That's really what it's all about. That's what any fraternity is about."

Stephen stared a moment, then he sent the ghost away and went back to the burgundy and back to the great ransacking of his house.

It was nearly ten when the doorbell rang. Stephen had filled a box, a trunk and two leaf bags with slivers and hunks of his past. He was working on the third bag when the bell broke through, like a signal, end of the first round. He opened the door for Tom Potter, fellow English teacher. Potter was a great fan and follower of James Joyce. He even looked like James Joyce, thin with thin white hair. He bowed slightly.

"Stephen."

Stephen answered in a very good Irish accent. "Well, now . . . it's Jimmy Joyce. Come in, Jimmy."

Potter stepped in and grimaced, as he stepped through the clutter on the floor.

"My god, Stephen. What *is* all this crap?"

"It's me life, Jimmy. Will ya help me toss it away?"

"Speak English, will you?"

He dropped the brogue. "Want some wine? Red. It's . . . no, it's empty."

"What's going on here?" Potter was stepping carefully about, his arms held close to his sides. "Was there an explosion?"

"Brandy. I have some Greek brandy, and we might as well finish it because I'm not taking it with me."

"Yes, I'll have a brandy, and *what* are you going to do with these enormous garbage bags? What's in them?"

"Ghosts, Jimmy." Stephen poured the brandy into coffee cups because they were closest.

"Will you drop the 'Jimmy,' please. Are you drunk?"

Stephen handed Potter his brandy. "No. No, I thought I would be by now, but this is very hard work. I've been sweating. Cheers."

Potter sipped, made a face. "Metaxa."

"Yes."

"Fiery stuff. I hate it." He stepped carefully to the couch, moved some papers, and sat down. "You really have made a mess, Stephen."

"The mess was here all the time, hiding. I've just . . . brought it out to look at it before I throw it all away."

"Mementos?" Potter asked, his eyes rifling through the scattered papers on the couch.

"Yes."

Doesn't he see them, Stephen thought. Doesn't he hear those voices? Elaine was doing her walk from the shower, walking right by Potter, and Randy was sitting next to him on the couch, a young man. Randy the child was lying on the floor. Elaine shouted from the kitchen, "Can you give me a hand?" and she stood at the door, leaving him forever.

"Mementos, Potter. . . . I thought we said our farewell at the farewell party. Why are you here?"

Potter didn't answer for a moment. He was staring at the folders on the coffee table. Among them were the folders that bore the names of the five men, and Stephen's heart caught when he saw that Potter was staring at them. Did he know the names? Would he recall? Potter was reaching out to straighten an old yellowed newspaper clipping in order to read it. Stephen felt an urge to rush to the table and snatch it away, then he thought, What's the difference? It doesn't matter. He would never guess what I'm going to do. And if he did? That wouldn't matter either. It was not something that could be stopped. Somewhere in the future, it was already done.

"You're reading about the trial of the five men who killed my son."

Potter recoiled from the clipping. "Oh, I didn't know, I . . ."

"Wasn't much of a trial. Went through the motions. Manslaughter, but everyone knew they'd be acquitted. It didn't matter to me. I have beer if you don't want the Metaxa."

"No, it's fine." He sipped, pensively. "It's just as well you're throwing all this stuff away."

Stephen sat on the coffee table. "Here's a picture of the five men."

Potter was nervous. "I heard about it. I wasn't here when . . ."

"Here's a small photo of Randy." It was in that same clipping. Potter glanced briefly, nodding, uncomfortable. Stephen stared at the photo, then looked up at Potter. A smile came to his face, surprising him. He almost said it. *Potter, I'm going to get them.*

"Jimmy, it feels good to finish, doesn't it? An end is such a gratifying thing to come to."

"You're well rid of that stuff. Start fresh. Start your traveling. Where did you say? Europe?"

"After I've seen some of the U.S. Why are you here, Jimmy?"

"Will you cut out the Jimmy crap?"

"Yes, Tom, why are you here? We already said goodbye. We shook hands. You grabbed my shoulder and said *bon voyage,* or was that West who. . . . What a swell party, wasn't it, Tom? Everyone left early, but not early enough for me." Stephen sipped the brandy and didn't like it either. Potter was staring at him, looking a little tense.

"Did you wish Margaret had stayed later?"

"Ah, Margaret . . ." Stephen drained the cup and threw it into one of the leaf bags. "That's why you're here."

"I saw how you two said goodbye."

"We kissed, as I remember. A quick one."

"I saw her eyes, Stephen."

"She cried, as I remember. Or at least she almost cried."

"She cried in the car going home."

"Some people do."

Potter was stiff, back straight, both hands gripping his coffee cup, and he was pale. "I want to know if you and Margaret were lovers."

"Oh, Jimmy, you ask me that . . . once a year."

"Don't call me Jimmy!"

Stephen sighed, his head bowing, shoulders stooping. He sat limply on the coffee table. Margaret Geary had been one of the very few in the last twenty years who had looked long enough at him so that he became solid and visible. Margaret saw. She touched. She reached inside of him for whatever might be found there. He had wondered too and waited. But she found nothing, brought nothing out of him. She had called him a man-in-waiting, and she had been right. Waiting for death, she said, but that was wrong. After that attempt, that dig that had turned up no treasure, they saw each other less. They made love, but she was no longer in love with him, only sad for him, and that's the look that Tom Potter had seen in her eyes. Only sadness. "No," Stephen said, "not lovers."

"I saw the way she looked at you."

Stephen studied him, growing impatient. In his mind he said, What do you care anyway? And he reached for Potter with an oversized, imaginary hand, but that hand stopped, hung there. "What do you care anyway?" Now he was actually shouting those words out loud. "Does it matter? What *is* she to you? Are *you* lovers?"

"That's not the point."

"What do you offer her? What do you trade her for her company? What?" Stephen was kicking through the rubble as he spoke, scattering papers and books and ghosts. "What?!"

Potter stood up. "I'm asking about *you!* You two!"

But Stephen wasn't listening. "You don't even make love, do you? You're so goddamn asexual. At least if you were gay, if you were something! . . ."

Potter was screaming, "You stop that crap! Stop it."

Stephen charged him, sticking out his hand, his real hand. "Sit down!" His hand didn't reach Potter, didn't have to. Stephen's large frame charging that way, Stephen Nye's heavy presence set into motion that way, created a force that pushed Potter back on the couch so hard that papers flew up in the air and the ghosts began to run and scream—all the Randys, all the Elaines.

"You have nothing to give!" Stephen was leaning over Potter now. "Jimmy Joyce is all you've got. You'd throw away Margaret, everybody, if only Jimmy Joyce would come out of the grave and put his arm around you and be your friend! You're as crazy with ghosts as I am! Oh, poor Margaret. My God! Two men full of nothing but ghosts!"

Potter was scrambling up to leave.

"Wait! Yes!" Stephen grabbed his arm. "Yes, we were lovers!"

Potter was afraid. He seemed about to cry. "You're crazy! You're drunk!"

"I'll show you!" Stephen pulled him across the room. "I'll show you the bed where we were lovers. Ten times, Jimmy! In . . . fifteen years. Ten times!"

"No!" Potter pulled with all his strength, couldn't tear his arm from Stephen's grip. "No!"

Stephen stopped, looked at the man twisting and pulling, the man who was held in the grip of Stephen Nye, the same Stephen Nye who had seldom raised his voice and never, never grabbed a man's arm in anger. He let go, and Potter stumbled through the rubble to reach the front door. Stephen followed him. "Go on, Jimmy! I've got more important things to do.

You want to know what?!" Potter was opening the door, fleeing, running. Stephen shouted after him, "You want to know what I'm going to do now!?" Then he slammed the door and turned to face the frightened, screaming, scurrying ghosts. He shouted at them. "Stop!"

All the Randys, all the Elaines, stopped and turned and stared at him with wide, frightened eyes. Then they slowly dissolved, disappeared. The house was quiet again, empty again, but for Stephen Nye.

He walked back into the living room and stood for a while. He felt tired, but good. He felt relieved, finally untangled from all this clutter around him. It meant nothing. It was garbage. He would throw it away just as he had thrown away Potter. Then he would be ready, and in the morning he would be gone, traveling light. He looked down at the coffee table. All that was important was gathered there: the folders bearing the names of the five men and the names of their children, the bus ticket to Madison, Wisconsin, where one of those children went to school—the first one.

4

B︴OB DAVIS slid into his favorite back booth in the
Uptown Coffee Shop. He was six-feet-four and
lean and he sprawled out now, pinching a menu
from the table next to his. When he leaned over to
read it, his elbows spread like wings and his knees
pressed on the table bottom. He ate his bacon and
three eggs, his arms and hands unattached, free
forms that floated over the food, salting, stabbing,

buttering. When he finished, he leaned back, and two tall shoes rose up on the bench opposite him, rested there, swaying back and forth like pendulums as he read his books.

Davis's parents were also tall and lean. His father had been the tallest of the five young men, had marched ahead of them through the forest, carrying Randal Nye's legs, holding them tight against his hips as Randal kicked and twisted and cursed and laughed.

"And there's Davis, studying away."

Bob smiled and drew in all his limbs, sat upright in the booth. Bonnie had spoken to him. She and a girlfriend were taking a table nearby, and he wanted to ask them to sit with him. He wrestled with that a moment. Maybe they were waiting for somebody.

"You're always studying, Davis."

It was Bonnie's friend, Chris, who was causing his confusion and shyness. She was black—lithe and lovely, her skin butterscotch colored and butterscotch smooth and maybe sweet to the taste. He imagined the touch of his lips to her neck, and his chest turned to stone. He couldn't breathe or swallow.

"Oh, why don't you two come and sit here if you're not . . . if you want. Okay?"

They did, and the talk eased into laughter. He put aside his heavy books on solemn high math. He let the morning grow dangerously close to his ten-o'clock class. He asked Chris about her home town, her major, and whether she liked chess.

"Davis is a chessman," Bonnie said.

"A king," Bob said. "No, a knight."

"I'm not very good at it," Chris said.

"Davis is a champ. Don't play him. Nobody beats him."

Chris smiled, tilting her head. "Is that true?"

Bob flushed with shy pride and shrugged, his shoulders launching upward, long neck bobbing forward. He glanced down at his hands on the table, saw his watch, saw his ten-o'clock class starting, saw his empty seat there.

"Hey, I have to go. Christ."

"See you in calculus, Davis."

"Yeah, bye. See you."

He was paying his check at the cash register and wondering if he should pay for the girls too. He could picture saying it—"Put their breakfast on my bill." But their check was already on the table and the waitress would have to go and get it and he didn't want to go through all the explanations and thank-yous and you're-welcomes.

It was then that he noticed the man. A large man alone in a booth, fairly well dressed, not old enough to be elderly really. Bob hardly looked at his face. He was staring at the small chess set on the table in front of the man.

He got his change from the cashier, waved goodbye to the girls and hurried outside, passing the restaurant window, glancing once more at the man playing chess by himself. He wanted to study the board. He pictured that, studying the board and then tapping on the glass, startling the man and shouting through the window, "Queen's knight to king's bishop four!" He smiled as he jogged to his ten o'clock, feeling high. He had spoken to Chris. She was nice. She played chess.

Bob had breakfast at the Uptown two days a week. The next time he went, he saw the man again, playing chess by himself, saw him through the window as he entered the restaurant. He went to his own back booth. All through breakfast he wondered if he should go introduce himself, maybe play him a game. But he didn't. He had his breakfast and read some math and paid his check. He did watch the man a moment, and caught his eyes as they came off the board. Bob and the man traded polite strangers' nods, polite smiles. Bob looked away, got his change, left. He thought he had seen something good in the man's look, a willingness for contact, an opening for friendship. He resolved that next time he saw the man, if he had time, if the girls didn't come in, he would ask to play him a game.

Bob watched her. She was far enough away, and she didn't see him, so he let himself really stare, really study her face, her breasts under the sweater, moving as she hurried down the library steps, her thighs under the short dress, working, shining like hand-rubbed wood, mostly her eyes, and they were hard to look at because she was turning now, moving toward him, seeing him. Her eyes changed when she saw him. Even before the smile he thought he saw his own feelings mirrored in her, and he wondered if she were feeling her chest turn to stone. Had she felt that before? Had she ever felt it because of a white boy?

He waved and walked to meet her. "Studying hard?"

She held up a book. "Ever read Lorca?"

"Poet. Yeah. No. I don't know."

"Really . . . tch. Just so fine."

"Spanish."

"Yeah. He's not even *required.* I just . . ."

"Study chemistry?"

"Ooh. No."

"Want to study out loud? We could meet in the Union and have a hamburger?"

"Tonight?" she said. And he suddenly imagined six, ten black men getting up off their chairs in some smoky room, turning to look at him, menacing men, their eyes narrowed and cold. She's ours. She's with us.

"Yeah." He shrugged. "I thought tonight, like about six, if you can. We could . . . say the formulas out loud. Quiz each other. As we eat. If you can."

"Okay."

The black men sat down out of sight and Bob smiled. "Good. Great." This one took about thirty seconds of hard thinking. His chest was pounding. "We could go to a show after if you want."

"Tonight?"

They jumped out of their chairs, the black men, rushed at him.

"If you want," he said quickly.

"Well," she said. She was quiet a while, and then she said such a strong, definite yes, that he knew he had won some very important battle in her mind. They had both won it.

Bob approached the Uptown Coffee Shop in a jog just because the morning was balmy and the sun was out. He jogged past the window where the man sat with his chessboard. Bob came through the door, hesitated, then walked to where the man sat, engrossed in his game, making a move then spinning the board around to the other side, studying. A flurry of opening lines rushed through Bob's mind. He blurted one.

"Hard to play yourself 'cause . . ."

The man looked at him, and smiled and the boy went on. "Cause you always know what your opponent is planning, y'know? You . . ."

The man said something, but the words were swallowed before Bob could hear them. "Pardon?"

"It's a challenge not to cheat." He extended a hand toward Bob. "Stephen Randal."

"Bob Davis." They shook hands. The man gestured to the opposite bench and Bob sat down.

"Don't let me interrupt your game."

The man arranged his small, pegged chessmen for a new game. "I hope you'll play one with me, if you have time."

"Sure. I've been meaning to ask you to play. I see you in here . . ."

"I know." The man was smiling at him again, a handsome man but crippled somehow, so unsure, so hungry for company. He moved the small board between them. "Please start."

Bob looked down at the board and became another person, a calm, steady, knowing Bob Davis, who moved in slow motion, his fingers gently lifting a chessman, carefully putting it in a new square, his eyes firm and fastened on the board. He had been playing since he was six. He was very good, and very pleased when he saw that this Stephen Randal could hold his own, give him a game. He hated to win too quickly. "You play well," Bob said, not looking up from the board.

"Well, I've been studying recently . . . preparing."

"Oh?" Now Bob looked at him. "For what?"

"For this game." There was silence. Then Bob Davis laughed out loud.

Bob played with intense concentration, forgot to order breakfast, hardly spoke. He was certainly beating the man, but it was taking him close to his ten-o'clock class.

"I'm sorry," Bob said. "It's getting late for me."

"Well, I'm almost beaten. Can we play again soon?" The man's manner was still shy and very friendly. Bob felt welcomed. "Thursday? Will you be here? We'll start earlier. Can you?"

"Sure, I'll be waiting," Stephen Randal said.

The next game was played more slowly. Bob let his mind slip off the board from time to time.

"What do you do, Mr. Randal?"

"Please. . . . Call me Stephen."

"All right."

The big man studied the board a while. Bob thought he was ignoring the question. Then Stephen spoke. "Retired teacher of English."

"Oh really? I'm lousy in English. I *like* it. I like *reading*. But it's hard for me to put my thoughts down. I'm a math major. What did you teach? I mean. . . . Literature?"

"Yes. Everything from . . . Ogden Nash to Jimmy Joyce." Stephen made a move which Bob had been expecting. Bob put Stephen into check. The man nodded his heavy head. "Mm. You've got me on the run."

"It wasn't easy."

"Well." Stephen sighed, "I'm still rusty. I just started playing again after . . . twenty years."

"Oh?"

"Yes. I used to play a lot with my son."

Ah, a son, Bob thought. He was starting to assemble a full picture of his new coffee-shop acquaintance. "I'll bet your son's a good player too."

"He's dead."

Bob kept his eyes on the board, wishing he could roll the conversation back, take out the last part. "I'm sorry." Stephen didn't respond, and in a moment Bob looked up at him. The old man was staring unfocused out the window. I'll bet he died in a war, Bob thought, and he tried to figure which one. Korea? Vietnam? He wanted to say It's your move, and bring Stephen back into the game, but he didn't. Then Stephen turned from the window and looked at him.

"Bob, I'd like to play you sometime when we're not so rushed."

Bob looked at his watch. "Right. I better go. Yes, I would too."

"I concede this one," Stephen said, arranging the pieces for a new game. "I know you're probably busy, with the weekend coming, but if there's an evening free, just come by the hotel—Mid-City Hotel. Around the corner there, on Hyatt. I'm there all the time. Just come by or call me."

Bob had a vision of a hotel of ancient drifters, sick old men, alcoholics. He tightened up a bit. "I just don't know my plans yet."

Stephen nodded. "No problem. I'll be there anyway. If you get a chance."

He seemed casual about it, not pushy, and Bob thought, He's probably lonely. The hotel might not be so bad. Maybe. . . . "Maybe, if I get a chance."

"Sure. It's Room Five-o-nine."

"Okay." Bob stood and they shook hands. "Room Five-o-nine."

Walking and talking, they had ambled a mile or more through the campus. Bob was carrying Chris's books and his own and still he was springing with each step, his heels thrusting him up another mile or more into the sky. His feelings for Chris made him buoyant, as if this new love were some great bubble inside of him. A jump would surely carry him over a building; a breeze would blow him across the street. They looked at each other and smiled, laughing as they walked. He wanted to touch the tan silk of her face or neck or hands. He felt his hand bumping hers, and he suddenly took it, held it. He looked far off, not breathing or swallowing. His right hand was the only part of him alive for the moment.

She left her hand in his, returned his grasp. He grinned as a gust of wind picked him up off his feet, carried him high above the campus, higher than the clouds. He held her hand tightly so she wouldn't fall.

Bob Davis was coming. The boy had just called. One hour. Stephen sat on the bed in his hotel room and tried to swallow, to breathe, to think. The son of William Davis would soon be in his room, in his reach.

He stood and went to the dresser, grabbed the folder marked DAVIS and stuffed it into a drawer. He leaned on the dresser top a moment, looked at himself in the mirror and wondered if he could do this, could really do this. He closed his eyes and told himself it was already done. One hour into the future he was doing it. Somewhere further in time he was finished with all five of them. Finished. "Finished," he whispered.

He stood straighter at the mirror and slowly raised his hands to his head. He smoothed his hair. He made his fingers try twice and three times to button the top button of his shirt, slide his tie into place. He went back to the bed and sat down to wait.

Bob Davis was startled by the person Bob Davis was becoming. Here he was, in love. Here he was, in love with a black girl. Here he was, on his way to meet an old gentleman for a chess game. This was his own old gentleman, not a grandfather or a friend of the family. This one belonged only to him and he was proud. He would introduce people to Stephen and speak of him in a letter home. Just a casual line. "I play chess once a week with a retired gentleman. We met in a café." Bob had always liked himself well enough, but he loved who he was becoming.

He jogged the last block to the hotel, stopped and looked at it. Ugly, old, but not nearly as bad as he expected. There may be families in there, women, not just hollow old men who coughed and drank and died. He went into the lobby. The place had once been fancy, maybe old Stephen was left over from the fancy days, or maybe he had come back here to stay a while in the old bridal suite he had shared with his wife. With that idea in his mind, Bob rode a slow, straining elevator to the fifth floor. He found 509 and knocked.

When Stephen opened the door, his face registered such deep emotion, Bob was suddenly off balance. The thought that someone in some small room in this city had been waiting with such hope and expectation for Bob Davis—it overwhelmed him. The man has no friends, Bob thought, no family, only the memory of his son, only chess, and me. He walked into Stephen's room feeling older. This new Bob Davis was maturing quickly. He took a box from under his arm, smiling at Stephen.

"Brought my favorite set."

"Oh, good, good. Here, sit here, Bob."

There were two old, worn, but comfortable easy chairs. They set up the chess game on a table between them, under a soft yellowy light. Stephen brought them glasses and poured red wine. Bob eased back into his new maturity, sipping burgundy and smiling at his new friend.

"Stephen. . . ." He liked using the first name of a man so old. "If you hadn't been playing chess, we never would have met."

Stephen settled back. The lamplight was gentle with his face. "That's why I was playing chess."

"Oh sure."

"I knew you were a champion."

Bob grinned. "Just by looking at me. Most people think I'm a basketball player. I hate basketball. Anyway, I'm glad we met." Stephen's smile was stretched thin. It trembled slightly but stayed in place. Bob sipped his wine. "You lived here in Madison all your life?"

"No."

"Where are you from?" But Stephen was studying him.

"Do you enjoy school, Bob? Do you have a lot of friends there?"

"Sure. I have a girl." She's black, he wanted to say, but of course he didn't. He would never toss it out like that, for effect. He did feel though that he and Stephen would someday discuss the racial thing. He would ask his friend Stephen's advice.

"Are you a member of a fraternity?"

Bob said, "No, I don't really care for 'em. They're okay for some guys. I just. . . . My dad had a really bad experience in a fraternity."

Stephen was very still, staring at him. "Yes?" His question was a whisper.

"They had an accident with a new guy, initiating a pledge, y' know? They didn't mean to hurt him, but the guy died."

Stephen whispered again. "How?"

Bob shrugged, "My Dad never wanted to go into it, y' know." Stephen's eyes left him, lost their focus. The man stared off a long time. "Shall we play now, Stephen?"

"Mm? Yes. Yes." Stephen's hand was unsteady, reaching for the wine bottle. He refilled their glasses. "This time you start."

Stephen nodded. "All right."

Stephen's smile came back and the evening glowed warm under the yellow lamplight. They finished the wine. Bob was a little high, a bit giddy, but it didn't affect his playing. He beat Stephen and they immediately set up for a new round.

"Are you warm?" Stephen said.

"A little."

"I'll tell you where I've been playing—but it's too cold now."

"Where?"

"On the roof," Stephen said. "I made an archaeological find on the roof." With a high nervous laugh he rose from his chair.

"A what?" Bob laughed.

"Really." Stephen sat on the bed and grabbed his knees to stop the shaking of his hands. "A neighbor on this floor showed me. There is a chessboard scratched into the cement of the roof."

"Oh . . ."

"Really. There is. Deep old gouges in the cement. We played up there. It's too cold now though, isn't it?"

Bob shrugged. "It's dark."

"We played in the dark."

Bob laughed again. "How?"

Stephen picked up a book of matches. "You never played this way?"

Bob sat up. "What way?"

Stephen lit a match. "You strike a match. The flame lights the board. While the match is lit you have to make your move—before it goes out. Before it burns your fingers!" Stephen laughed loudly and seemed to shiver. They both laughed. "You don't believe me. I'll show you the chessboard on the roof."

Stephen was rising, leaving the lamplight, and going to the door. Bob was still chuckling at the whole idea, trying to get out of the chair.

"Bring the chessmen," Stephen said. "We'll play up there."

"That's crazy." Bob realized he was a little dizzy from the wine and that made him laugh even more. "Wait, Stephen."

"Come on, I'll show you."

Stephen was gone. The door was open. Bob was picking up chessmen, dropping them, swearing and laughing. He put all the men in his pockets. Then he saw, on the table, the book of matches. He laughed harder. "Stephen." He put the matches in his pocket and went out the door. Stephen was at the end of the hallway, holding open the door to the fire escape, yelling in a whisper.

"Come on, Bob."

Bob followed, chuckling and shaking his head. "You even forgot the . . ."

But Stephen was gone again, moving ahead of him up the fire-escape steps, up to the roof. Bob was outside now, and the cool air felt good, so did the exertion of climbing the metal stairs. He stepped onto the gritty roof, saw Stephen walking ahead of him.

"Stephen, you even forgot the matches."

But Stephen was moving quickly across the roof, turning as he walked. "Come on. It's here."

Bob followed, washed by the cold wind, still laughing. "Stephen, it's too windy for matches."

But Stephen stood at the roof edge now, pointing to a spot on the low wall of the roof. "It's here," he said.

Bob walked to him, smiling. In the darkness it seemed as though Stephen wasn't smiling at all. He looked frightened. His hand trembled, pointing to the wall. "Here. It's right here."

Bob put a hand on his shoulder, felt that the old

man was shivering. "Stephen, it's too windy for matches."

"Look!" Stephen was pointing, shouting at him. "Here!"

Bob took a step toward the low wall of the roof, studying the top of the wall. There were no deep gouges there, no chessboard, nothing.

Then he was suddenly sucking in the cold wind and falling. His long arms went out like thick ropes, lifelines reaching incredible distances through black space and touching nothing. His long legs were spread too. He was a giant stick figure twirling down through darkness.

Ellen fell backward, knocked over an end table and sat there on the floor, shaken. Ann hurried in from her room, shouting something that the music drowned out.

"Christ sake, Ellen! You shouldn't dance in here. You all right? You're going to wreck the place and break your neck." She came close to Ellen, put out a hand to help her up, but Ellen didn't take the hand, didn't look at her. "Are you all right?"

"Something happened. I got dizzy."

"Well, get up."

"No."

Ann marched back into her room, mumbling.

Ellen added, mostly to herself, "I don't get dizzy."

She had been sweating, and now she was suddenly very cold. She wore only panties and a T-shirt and she drew her legs up, hugged her knees. She shivered. I guess I'm getting sick, she thought, not really believ-

ing it. It was something else, a feeling. In a minute it
went away. She was all right, only scared.

When Bob Davis had stood close to him on the
roof, Stephen's body had been quivering, nearly out
of control. But when the boy took his step to the roof
wall, Stephen's arms had come up swiftly, with
strength and purpose, and they had pushed forward
exactly as they did in the dream. Instead of thrusting
his arms forward through the flames to save Randal,
he had thrust them through the darkness of the
rooftop. He had connected with the body of Robert
Davis and *pushed*.

Stephen had heard the boy strike the alley and
break there. He had turned to hurry to his room,
fighting panic, getting his suitcase, moving on. He
was in a cab now, heading for the bus station.
Everything was in motion. Somewhere in Madison,
Wisconsin, somebody was on his way to that alley.
That someone would find the boy and call the police.
The police would call the boy's father and the first of
the five men would come face to face with his fate,
with the end of that inescapable circle he helped
begin twenty years ago. By that time, Stephen Nye
would be on his way to the second child.

He sat back in the cab and tried to quiet his heart.
His mind kept screaming questions at him—Did it
really happen? Have you really done it? He suddenly
thrust his hands forward, his arms out stiff in front of
him. Yes. He had done it. He remembered the feel of
Bob Davis's back against his hands. It wasn't rubber.
It was real.

The voice inside asked again, Are you sure? and Stephen laughed at that voice. He laughed and wept with release. He had been listening to that screaming doubt all his life. You can't, it would say. Not *you.* You'll never balance on a two-wheel bike. You'll fall. You think you'll ever be able to drive a car? You? You'll never enter a woman. You'll fail. You'll never raise your hands against anyone. Not you. He smiled and felt tears on his face. He choked that doubting voice, and it died.

5

"MR. WILLIAM DAVIS?"

"This is . . . yes, speaking."

"Mr. Davis, this is Officer Cole of the Madison Police Department. Do you have a son, Robert, attending the university here?"

"Yes, I do. Wha . . ."

From that second to this one, three hours later,

William Davis's heart had not let loose of him. It battered his chest, throbbed inside his ears. The phrases "dead on arrival" and "a fall from a building" had been muted, faraway. None of it had mattered after that first second of knowing. The boy was gone. Robert, Bob, Bobby—the gawky, growing thing that was still beginning had somehow ended.

William Davis was driving too fast, streaking through the morning, just now crossing from Illinois into Wisconsin. He would be in Madison soon, someplace he didn't want to go. He didn't want to claim the body, make "arrangements," drive back home, live out the next days and weeks.

He pressed harder on the gas pedal. He wanted to drive into next year. He wanted to get somewhere and stop the car and get out and Bobby would be dead a year, and then, maybe, he could breathe a normal breath, think a whole thought. Maybe then he could let loose the memories of his son. He had them in a nailed-down box now, under a shelf in a dark corner of his mind. If just one of those memories got out and whispered to him or smiled at him, he would die, he knew, he would drive off the road into a tree.

He realized his hands were clenched tightly on the steering wheel, but he didn't relax them. He couldn't relax any part of himself because he was fighting every minute against the waves of sorrow, waves of fear, waves of fury.

On a morning one week later, Chris Williams was passing the Uptown Coffee Shop, and she stopped, remembering. Her friend, Di, saw in Chris's eyes that she was with Bob Davis again. Di was black also, and she had never met Bob, but she hated him for being white and for loving Chris and then dying.

"Come on, don't stop."

But Chris was moving toward the restaurant entrance. "I want some coffee."

They took a table far from where Chris had sat with Bob, but it was still all in her eyes anyway, and all the words were still in her brain. Right then she was seeing Bob shrug. Bonnie was calling him a chess champion and he was shrugging.

"I told you it would be grief," Di said. "You said a white boy and I said grief. First word out of my mouth." Di was angry at everyone white and at death and this coffee shop and at herself because she was helpless—just sitting and stirring her coffee and watching Chris's eyes fill up with memories and start to overflow.

"Goddamn it, Chris. Shit."

"I can't help it. He was . . . nice."

Di leaned across the table. "The nice ones get trampled by the big crowd of assholes. Jesus Christ! It was probably some redneck asshole who couldn't stand to see him with a black girl so he took him up to that roof. . . . Oh my God, Chris, I'm sorry."

But Chris was frozen a moment, staring in horror, not at Di but at Di's idea, at the possibility that it might be true. It might very well be true.

"I'm sorry, honey, please. It didn't happen that way. I just . . ."

But Chris was covering her mouth so she wouldn't scream at the sight of those arms, hands, fingers stretched tight and pushing, pushing her Bob off the world as a voice said, "That'll teach *you*. That'll teach *her*," and a face, the face of all hate, nightmare face of all evil, twisted back at her. "That'll teach *you*. That'll teach *her*."

Three weeks later, a morning on the campus of the University of Missouri was just losing its early chill, just chiming through eight o'clock, just finding its pace. It moved at a walk, except that Tom Johns was running. He ran three miles a day, through the campus, across a park, back again to his fraternity house. Running kept his trim, tight body in shape, made him a better soccer player, but actually he ran for the fun of running.

When he ran, he was the only thing alive. Trees were just stones, measuring his miles, and people were just trees, shapes to jog around. He felt like an ancient god doing a quick inspection, examining each day when it was still wet and new, giving it his okay.

Sometimes he sang songs to the rhythm of his run, silently making the words in his mind. If he happened to see a woman who was worthy, he might give her his attention for a moment, undressing her as he passed by, then turning to glance at her face, and, if she were beautiful, maybe he would run backward a moment or jog in place as he smiled, flirted, tried to pick her up.

"You're beautiful. Want to run with me?"

He had gotten a date that way last month, but she had turned out to be only mortal after all, and he hadn't bothered to call her back. He had envisioned god and goddess making love in the heavens, reaching sublime positions in the night sky and having constellations named after them. She had expected courtship, wouldn't mate on the first date, mundane mortal. He made a mental note to call her that night. He would give her one more chance at becoming a constellation.

He shined a big grin at the lady with the baby. He saw her almost every morning outside the married students' housing. She smiled, and he was sure she lusted for him. She was trapped in married students' housing with a husband and a baby, and Tom Johns was free, as well as handsome, and his body rippled as he ran. Someday he might snatch her up into his arms and just keep running. The husband would shout, baby would cry, but the mother would love it. He knew it was what she dreamed about. He would run with her into the park, tear off her housecoat and give her his body in such glorious intercourse that she would go mad from too much pleasure. And he would just keep running.

He passed the two fags he always passed. They were late for class today. He nodded. They nodded. He knew they wanted him too. After he had passed them, he was sure they were staring after him, delighted with his body.

He trotted into the park and waved at the old couple seated on the bench they always sat on. They lusted after him too, he knew, because he was young and quick. He made them ache with desire for the past. He made them hate their ancient bodies. He was sure of it.

56 | GERALD DiPEGO

He turned to wave at the other old man, but he wasn't there. For the first time in weeks, the big tall man wasn't standing among the trees, watching him run by. The man had appeared about a month ago, had been there every day, watching him, smiling slightly, sometimes waving. He also desired Tom Johns, Tom thought, not for his body, not for his youth, for something else. It was as if he wanted the boy to stop and talk, to connect with him. But Tom Johns just kept running. Once he had turned and seen the big man still watching him.

Tom ran up a hill and onto a small dirt road that brought him above the park. He searched again, but the old man wasn't there. He ran on, almost in darkness now because the trees were so thick along the road. It was his tunnel, he called it, and he knew that in forty-four strides he'd be out of the tunnel and back on the street.

At the seventeenth stride he heard the car—so strange to hear an engine sound from within the trees. Eighteen. Nineteen. That car was roaring, peeling out. Twenty. The car came through a clearing in the trees, came zooming out onto the dirt road, came at him.

He turned in mid-stride, so surprised. He saw things very clearly—the front of the car looming at him, oversized, giantlike, and beyond it a face stretched tight, teeth uncovered, eyes wide. It looked like the big old man; and what was he doing here? Tom's mind was asking that question as the car smashed his body and ended his life.

Stephen Nye, seated alone at a booth in a dark bar, slid his hands outward on the table top, slowly thrust them forward until his elbows were locked and his arms were out stiff in front of him. His hands had been thrust out that way each time he had rushed into the flames in the dream of Randal, and they had been in the same position when he pushed Robert Davis off the roof, and this morning they had been locked that way on the steering wheel as he drove the car into Thomas Johns.

The dream was not just a dream, he decided. It had always been a signal of what was coming, a preview. His rush to save Randal was really his attack on the children of the five young men. It was the same motion. He had been powerless to save his son. The boy had died a hundred miles away from him. But he *had* the power to strike back, to deliver the awful fate to each of the five. All he had to do was lift his arms, stretch them forward, the power was there.

"You want another?" The waitress appeared out of shadow.

"Yes." He watched her walk away. He had been watching her for an hour. She wore a black outfit, low-cut and short, barely covering her buttocks, and black net stockings. Her body was attractive, but not vulnerable. It was armor, fending off all the thousands of glances and stares. He looked at her thighs and her ass beneath the black net, but his looks just bounced off. Now, as she turned to bring him a fourth glass of wine, he ignored her body and went for her eyes. As she came close, she glanced down, away from him, and for the first time he felt he was stronger than she.

"Thank you," he said. "What's your name?"

"Danny."

"For Danielle?"

She smiled and seemed to weaken a bit. "Just a nickname."

"I just drove in from Columbia. There a good hotel around here?"

She shrugged. "The Admiral."

He nodded. "Come there with me." He hadn't planned that, and it shocked him. He had never dared to do this before.

She let out a little incredulous laugh, not mocking, just surprised. "No thanks." She left quickly, back to business.

Nye took a deep breath and toasted the moment, sipped the red wine, proud of himself for trying. What if she had said yes? He imagined that little laugh of hers, followed by, "All right. I get off in an hour." He imagined making love. He hadn't done it in four years and hadn't really wanted to, until lately. The hunger had come back. He didn't question his performance. Tonight he had the power. He toasted himself again. A murder and a woman in one day. That would have been something.

A few minutes later he went to the bathroom and realized the wine was taking over. His head felt empty, balance wasn't there. He stared at himself in the mirror. He slowly raised his hands, thrust them out in front of him, looked at his eyes, looked deep into the power.

He had been back at his booth for ten minutes when she entered the bar. The waitress must have told the bartender about Stephen's pass, and he must have called this woman. She questioned the bartender with a look, and he nodded toward Stephen. She came toward him, his first whore.

"Hello there," she said, and she didn't size him up, didn't examine. She just smiled. "You drinking alone tonight?"

Stephen smiled back, not at her, at the idea of it—a murder and a woman in one day.

She was overripe, Stephen thought, hair and lips over-red, make-up overdone, body soft, but what a good present for himself, and not very expensive. Oh, how he could cuddle in all that softness. He could swim in it. He decided he would pay her ten dollars more than she asked.

"It's twenty-five, hon. I'll stay with you an hour if you like." She was so professional. "You just passing through Saint Louie? You a businessman, or what?"

"I just drove in from Columbia. I had an accident there this morning and it shook me up a bit. *You* drive, okay?"

"Sure, hon. Was anybody hurt?"

"My car was dented. It's a rented car. I suppose I'm in trouble."

She shook her head. "Nah, insurance'll take care of it."

"Oh, I'm in trouble, all right." He laughed aloud, and she laughed, too.

They drove to a motel and didn't register at all. She had a key to a room, small but clean and pleasant. Stephen was giddy, eager to watch her undress, to feel her nakedness under the sheet.

She put only the bathroom light on and half-closed

the door so that the bedroom was dim. "You want to talk, hon?"

"No." He sat on the bed, half working at his shoes, mostly watching her. She was neat with her clothes, folding her blouse and skirt on a chair. She wore sheer pantyhose with nothing underneath and Stephen's hands got ready for that ass. His erection began. She undid her bra and he smiled, his hands aching to hold her large soft breasts. He was hurrying out of his clothes, his erection nearly complete now and getting in the way.

She was under the covers first. When he slid beside her, felt the cold sheet and her warm softness, his penis stretched until it hurt with a glorious pain. He hadn't had an erection so full in years, or maybe never, never this strong.

"What do you like, hon?"

"Shhh." Stephen was letting himself get lost. He closed his eyes and put his arms around her, put his legs around her. "Shhh." He hugged her tight, rolled her on top of him, his organ squeezed between their bellies. His hands went to that ass and stroked and then grabbed. She gave him an encouraging moan, but he was already over the edge, lost. He rolled them over again, on top of her now, his legs working to spread hers.

"Hon?"

But he was already probing with his organ, finding where her flesh gave and then pushing.

"Hon, wait . . ."

Then she gasped as he went inside. She was trying to move under him, to adjust, to eliminate the pain, but he was heavy on her and strong.

He went very deep inside her and brought his knees up, rose up to balance on his knees as his hands came around to her breasts and took them. He was somewhere outside of consciousness. His body rose higher and moved farther back as his arms straightened out in front of him. He locked his elbows, his arms stiff, his hands pushed forward as in the dream, as in the murders. He was full of the power.

He closed his long, strong fingers on her breasts, his arms shaking. He pulled that tender flesh toward his face. He closed his eyes and saw breasts yards long, stretching like rubber toward his mouth. He felt skin soft as suede brush his lips. He opened his mouth and closed his teeth on the nipple of her breast. It was real. It was all real. She cried out. "Wait! DON'T!" But Stephen was coming inside of her in great surges of power, and his hands squeezed her, and his teeth clenched tight on her. Her eyes closed and her mouth opened wide, only a whimper came out as she moved her head from side to side, as her hands pulled at his hair.

He made a sound like a deep hum, his body quivering, his teeth locked on that softness. She breathed in and wailed in a high voice, her eyes closed, her head flung from side to side.

When he was empty, he lay on her, his body going loose. She moved away, turned on her face, and wept into the pillow.

He felt far away from her, too far to go, too far to talk. He listened to her crying, so far away.

She was trying not to cry too loudly. Her hand moved up to touch her breast and she pressed her face into the pillow to catch her cries. She lay there for ten minutes, in tears, in pain, hating him. She decided she wouldn't scream at him what she wanted to scream or kick him where she wanted to kick. He was probably one of those crazy ones. He might hurt her more. He was strong.

She got out of the bed, crying quietly now. She dressed quickly, didn't try to put her bra on, shoved it into her purse. She glanced at him and the bastard was watching her, his eyes almost closed but still watching her.

Stephen closed his eyes, already half into sleep, crossing the rest of the way now as he heard the door click shut, as he realized he hadn't given her the extra ten dollars.

THE PARENTS of Tom Johns were speaking quietly with two detectives in the Columbia, Missouri, Municipal Building. The room they were in was so spare it seemed empty. The people were hushed, issuing a quiet word or phrase now and then.

A shoe scraped on the floor.

A detective turned a page.

Mrs. Johns sighed.

"They're typing it now. You can sign it and go," one detective said. The other added, "Just take a minute."

Mr. Johns nodded. A third detective came in and all four people turned to him. He sat on the edge of the table, studied Mr. and Mrs. Johns a moment before he spoke.

"We've been examining the tire marks." He studied them a bit longer. "Looks to me like the driver was waiting for somebody to come by."

Mrs. Johns said, "Oh, my God . . . on purpose?"

The detective nodded, went on. "He really peeled out of there. The vehicle struck your son, then went on through shrubs, hit a tree and left some paint—metallic gray. We're asking everyone in the area if they saw an auto of that description, and we'll be checking the body shops." He paused. "Please, now . . . take your time and try to think of anyone who might possibly want to harm your son."

They thought. In the long silence, Mrs. Johns shuddered. The things in the room seemed to be losing shape and color, dissolving. Then Mr. Johns said, "Nobody."

Later that night, on a plane from St. Louis to Cincinnati, Mr. Johns's mind traveled a crooked path toward Stephen Nye. He connected the death of his son with the death of Randal Nye—but only in the sense of irony, terrible irony. He looked at the window which only reflected himself, and he spoke his wife's name. "Irene?" He felt her, heard her turn to him. "Something happened to me in college. I never told you about it."

He told her the story of Randal Nye, the awful

accident. It was another case of death coming unexpectedly to a young boy at school. Irene held his arm, put her head on his shoulder. They both thought of the terrible irony of it.

A week later Irene answered her phone to hear the voice of the third detective again.

"Mrs. Johns, we've located the car. Found it in a body shop in Saint Louis. It was a rented car, rented to a Stephen Nye. Does the name mean anything?"

She thought, then stiffened. "Nye? *Nye!*?"

The third detective's name was Holcomb. From Mr. Johns, he learned the story of Randal Nye and got a list of four names. He called the Alumni Association of Northern Illinois University and the National Office of Sigma Delta Fraternity. He got addresses for each of the four men, very old addresses in some cases. Then he called the homicide divisions of the police departments in each of the four cities. He told the whole story four times. In Chicago, the detective on the other end of his call was Sergeant James Dela.

Dela was taking notes, trying to hold on to his temper, failing.

"Wait a minute. Now wait a fucking minute. You've got the name and address of this guy in Chicago, this intended victim, and you're taking your goddamn time about filling me in, and you haven't even *called* this guy yet? Wait a minute." Dela put the receiver against his chest and shouted. "Bridge!"

Detective Bridger looked up from his newspaper. He was a large black man, strong and solid as the desk he had his feet resting on.

"What?"

"Move your ass and call a Daniel T. King who works at Cal-Vy. That's C-a-l-dash-V-y Sporting Equipment on Wabash, and tell him to go home and gather his family and lock his doors. He may be in danger, and I'll call him and fill him in as soon as I get rid of this Missouri asshole." Back to the phone. "Okay, Missouri, what else have you got on Stephen Nye? Yeah? He rented the car in his own name? Christ. Why don't I have a picture of him on my desk right now? Wait a minute." He put the phone on his chest again. "Leo!"

Detective Leo Small was walking by, trying not to burn his fingers with a very full cup of coffee. "What the hell you got there, Dela?"

"A fucking psycho. Call Iverson, Illinois, and get everything you can on a Stephen Nye. That's N-y-e, a retired teacher from Iverson Junior College. Get pictures." Back to the phone. "Okay, Missouri, you have the date of the death of this guy's son . . . Randal? . . . Not the *year*, the goddamn *day*. Jesus. Look, just because he already wasted the one in *your* town, does that mean you can get sloppy? This old fart could be pulling the trigger on my citizen right now. . . . Wonderful. . . . Same to you. . . . Yeah, go home and plow your north forty. What is this, you guys work half days at harvest time?" He slammed the phone down. "Goddamn shitkicker. Bridge! You get that Daniel King?"

"Cal-Vy Sporting Equipment."

"Mr. Daniel King, please."

"One moment, please."

"Mr. King's office."

"I'd like to speak to Mr. King."

"May I say who's calling?"

"Detective Bridger, Police Department."

"One moment."

"Hello?"

"Mr. Daniel T. King?"

"Yes."

"Mr. King, this is Detective Lyle Bridger of the Chicago Police Department."

"Is anything wro . . . ?"

"We're just getting briefed on a case that concerns you, Mr. King, and we wanted to warn you of a possible danger to you and your family."

"What is this?"

"I don't have all the facts, they're coming in long distance to another detective and he'll fill you in. Meanwhile, go home, gather your family, make sure the door is locked."

"Well, now wait a minute, Jesus . . ."

"Just a moment, Mr. King. I'm putting him on."

"Hi, Daniel King?"

"Yes, wha . . . ?"

"This is Detective Sergeant James Dela. I just got a call from Columbia, Missouri, concerning a homicide there. Do you recall an . . . Edward Johns?"

"Johns?"

"You knew him in college."

"Ed Johns, yes, I. . . . He was killed?"

"His son was murdered and we think the man responsible is Stephen Nye—"

"I don't understand this. Jesus."

"—the father of Randal Nye, a boy from your fraternity at Northern Illinois Uni . . ."

68 | GERALD DiPEGO

"Oh Jesus oh my God no."

"So far we believe this Stephen Nye has killed the son of Edward Johns and the son of . . . William Davis, a couple of months ago."

"Oh . . . I. . . . Oh, God . . ."

Mr. King was suddenly, unexpectedly crying, and Dela waited a moment.

"Do you have a son, Mr. King?"

"No, I . . . I have no children. I'm . . . Just my wife and I . . ."

"Call her, then go home. Stay home, and I'll see you both in about . . . three hours. Okay?"

"My God, this is . . . I'm sorry, I just . . ."

Dela waited a moment.

"All right, Mr. King. My name is Dela, D-e-l-a. Take down the number. Two-two-four, o-seven-nine-one. Got it?"

"Yes."

"Now, call your wife; go home; stay there. If you need me, call. I'll see you in about three hours. All right?"

"Yes."

"Okay." Dela hung up, took a long breath. He flashed a map of the U.S. in his mind, made big red dots at Madison, Wisconsin, and Columbia, Missouri, at L.A. and Chicago and New York. Chicago was next, Dela thought. This guy, this geriatric, psychotic asshole was on his way to Chicago, or he was already here.

Somewhere under that big red dot Dela had placed over Los Angeles, Ellen Skate was dancing. She was dancing alongside Tony, a young man from the studio she attended, but actually, she was dancing with Herbie Mann. Her eyes were closed and she was living inside the music that crashed out of the stereo speakers, dancing inside the notes, inside the flute of Herbie Mann.

Her movements were small and sensuous. She was almost liquid, her body pouring down from a raised arm, through her rippling back, into melting hips that washed from side to side and then oozing down into her thighs. She ended on her knees, head bowed, long hair like a black puddle on the floor.

"Really, really good, El!"

"I was gone."

"Really nice."

Then the album's next song began, and Ellen and Tony were kicking high and arching their backs, wild marionettes, their strings attached to the sticks of Herbie Mann's drummer.

They were in Ellen's living room with the furniture pushed back to give them room. It was warm and they had already shed some clothes. Both of them down to T-shirts and cut-offs, and now, in rhythm, Tony was stripping off his sweaty shirt, making his moves part of the dance.

Ellen liked the moves, and she did the same, slipping out of her shirt in perfect time to the music, trailing it from her hand for a while like a scarf, then tossing it away. She wore no bra, felt no modesty with Tony, not here anyway, in the middle of the music. They felt their bodies grow lighter. Tony undid his cut-offs, so did she. They both kicked off their denim shorts on the beat. Ellen's fingertips entered the waistband of her panties and spread the elastic, began slowly working the cloth down, moving her hips to the drumbeats, sliding the material down over the curve of her buttocks, down her thighs. She danced away, leaving the last of her clothes on the floor. Tony did the same. They were flying on top of the tempo, smiling, in perfect sync.

When the tune ended, they froze, waiting. No self-conscious laughter broke through. They waited, naked, breathing hard, ready to fly on the downbeat. The next piece began, and they were dancing again, more slowly now, improvising moves that slipped them deeper and deeper into the music. Neither of them heard the front door open.

Ann stood in the doorway, immobile except for her eyes and mouth, which were opening wide. She walked in and slammed the door behind her. "Jesus Christ! Ellen!"

Ellen and Tony stopped, looked at Ann, looked at each other and smiled, a bit embarrassed now.

"What the hell are you doing!?"

"Ann, this is Tony," Ellen said, and she started dancing again.

"Hi, Ann," Tony said.

Ann advanced on them, rumpled, sandy and sunburned from a day at the beach. She wore a short beach coat with her bikini underneath. She threw her car keys down. "Are you two drunk or stoned?!"

"We're just dancing, Ann," Ellen said.

Ann went quickly to the record player and turned it off. "Then dance in your room with the door closed, for God's sake!"

"I've had people dancing with me here before."

"Not naked!" When Ann said that her voice went shrill, and Ellen suddenly laughed, and then covered her mouth. Tony had picked up his underwear. Now he stopped, wondering what was next.

Ann screamed, "It's not funny!"

"Look at *you*. You're almost naked."

"*I am not naked!*" They stared at each other for a moment, and Ellen wouldn't have done it if she hadn't seen that smile threatening to break on Ann's face. She lunged, reaching under the beach coat. Ann stepped back and let out a great shrill whoop when she realized what Ellen was doing, but it was too late. Ellen's fingers had already found Ann's bikini bottom and were yanking it down. Ann tried to pull away, but the bottoms were around her knees by then, and she fell.

As Ann fell, her legs rose up and Ellen pulled the bottoms off her feet and tossed them away. Ann sat up, her face on fire with sunburn, anger, and embarrassment. "Goddamn it, Ellen!"

"Join us, Ann," Ellen said.

Tony smiled, putting the music on. "Come on, dance with us."

"Bastards!" Ann rose, holding the beach coat around her and heading for her room. When she heard and felt Ellen run after her, she screamed, "No!" and sprinted for her door. Ellen might have let her go, except that within Ann's scream she had heard a hint of laughter.

Ellen caught her at the closed door. The beach coat was unbuttoned, and Ellen grabbed it, pulled it back and down over Ann's shoulders. Ann whooped again and struggled out of the coat, ran for her door. This time Ellen caught her by the bikini top, and the material gave. Ann stumbled against the door and slid down to the floor, in a tug-of-war with Ellen over her last bit of clothing. She was bigger and stronger than Ellen, but she was starting to cackle, and her laughter weakened her. She couldn't tighten her fists around her bikini top, and it slipped away. She screamed and kicked and cursed and couldn't stop laughing. It was as though Ellen had stripped years from her along with her clothes, ten years at least. Ann was laughing at the idea of being naked, at the sight of her own nipples and crotch, at the sight of her nude roommate and a nude young man smiling at her and dancing. Ann was a giggling ten-year-old who had stripped down in mixed company to enjoy a garden sprinkler.

Ellen took her hand and tried to stand her up. Ann pulled back, sitting down and covering her body and laughing through her cursing.

"Come on, dance with us."

"Jesus, Ann, you might as well."

"You're both a couple of perverts!" Ann shouted, and all three of them laughed. Then Ann got to her feet and began to move a little to the music, still covering up, still laughing.

"Come on, dance!"

And they did, Ellen and Tony giving themselves totally to the music and Ann more tentative, still flushed red, still getting the giggles and having to stop now and then to cover her face. They danced through two songs. In the middle of the third, the doorbell rang and Ellen danced over to open it.

"Don't open it!" Ann ran for her room as Ellen opened the door.

A middle-aged man stood in the doorway, staring

at Ellen, at the naked boy dancing behind her, at the bare-assed girl running across the room.

Ellen's mouth dropped open, and she slammed the door and turned to the others. "Oh fuck, it's my father."

From her room Ann screamed, "Oh no!" Tony sat on the floor, his side aching from dancing and laughing.

Ellen put her back against the door and rolled her eyes to the ceiling, shouted through the door. "Daddy, are you still there?"

"Yes, Ellen . . ."

"Wait!" She turned the record off. "Get dressed," she whispered to Tony, and she shouted another "Wait!" at her father. Tony was having trouble dressing. He was still laughing, his shorts half on. Ellen pushed him and he went hopping on one foot into her room. She closed the door and came through the living room, gathering her clothes, slipping them on. She opened the door, her face apologizing and not knowing what to expect. "Dad, we were just dancing, that's all. When you dance with your clothes off . . ." She stopped because of his expression. He was not at all angry, but much more shaken than she had expected, and in his eyes there was a sadness she couldn't explain. She spoke much more softly. "Dad . . . nothing bad happened. You just caught your daughter dancing nude, like the ancient Greeks used to do . . . when they were young Greeks."

He could barely speak. "I tried to call."

"I leave it off the hook when I dance. Dad, I . . ."

"I don't care, baby," he said. "I'm just glad you're

okay. Now you have to come with me. Pack some clothes and come with me. You have to go out of town for a while."

Ellen felt dread then, got another chill, another feeling of something about to happen. Maybe it had happened. "Is Mom all right?"

"Yes. Everybody's all right. We're going to meet her now . . . out of town. I'll tell you on the way."

"Are you in trouble, Daddy?"

"I'll tell you on the way."

Ann stayed in her room, embarrassed. Tony left quickly. Frank Skate waited in the living room while his daughter packed.

Ellen packed hurriedly, excited, secretly glad there was some kind of trouble because it had brought her father swooping into her life, caring about her, taking charge, giving her a direct order. Ellen's life up to now had been spent mostly on the fringe, just on the rim of the circle, looking in on a mother whose attention was elsewhere, looking for a father who was just passing through. She felt at the center of something, she didn't know what.

Frank Skate waited until he was off the freeways and driving south along the coast. "I swear to God. Half the people in this world are sick. More than half."

"Dad."

"Seventy percent, easy."

"Please tell me what's happening."

But he didn't speak for a while. He stared at the road, feeling as if he were holding up a cracked and leaning wall. It pressed down on him. If he let go, it would fall and break. It was a wall built of responsibilities, bad debts, his business, his wife, and now this. Now a sick old man from twenty years ago was up there sitting on the wall.

The wall trapped him. He lived his life in one-hand grabs and mad dashes, stealing a weekend, spending a day in bed, not thinking or worrying or caring for six hours, then hurrying back to catch that wall before it fell and broke on the ground.

He had an image of escape. Escape was piloting a small plane, a seaplane, and flying it along the coast and among the islands of British Columbia, skipping from one island to the next like a flat stone. He had flown such a plane for one day. He remembered the tops of fir trees. He remembered eagles and the absence of other men. "And this country is the sickest. I'd kiss it goodbye in a minute if I could." His hands pulled back slightly on the steering wheel, lifting his car off the road, flying it up through the clouds to look for the sun.

"Would you take me with you?"

He glanced at his daughter, his girl grown somehow to eighteen. She had just asked him a question. He wasn't sure what it was.

"Would you, Dad?"

She was part of the wall, part of the trap. He liked her, loved her, and he wished she could always be safe and happy and somewhere far away from him. He wished they were all far away, and he was alone, over Canada. "Would I what?"

His expression answered her question. She turned to the road. "Never mind. Tell me what's happening."

Frank nodded, staring ahead a moment, his big

broad Cadillac whipping down the coast. "All right, listen and don't interrupt." He drove in silence for another few moments.

"Dad!"

"All right! I'm thinking! Now listen."

"I promise I'll listen for Christ's sake. Talk."

"Twenty years ago, Ellen . . ."

"Oh, Jesus . . ."

"Now listen! Twenty years ago I was a student at Northern Illinois. I was in a fraternity."

"Joe College."

"We decided to really *get* the pledge class. They had raided the house, messed it up. You know what I mean? Pledge class—the kids being initiated into . . ."

"Yeah, go ahead."

"We decided we'd grab one and take him way out someplace, not just drive him out of town . . . way out." Skate's eyes stayed on the road but they were slightly glazed, covered by layers of time, twenty years. "We decided we'd take him out into the woods and tie him up. At night, y' know. Then we'd call the other pledges and tell them, 'All right we've got one of you. He's in the woods north of Weyland's farm'— that's where we finally took him. Anyway, then the pledges would have to find their man and free him. Might take them all night, we figured." He paused, living it again.

"So?"

"So we planned the whole thing, and we picked our target. Randal Nye. He was the easiest. He was hanging around the fraternity house a lot, like he was waiting . . . hoping to be hassled. He was eager for it, y' know. Sometimes we'd grab a few pledges, make 'em clean the place, do calisthenics, crazy things. Nye loved it. He was eager, just . . . Anyway, we planned the night, the time. I said I'd get some handcuffs."

"Handcuffs?"

Here Frank Skate's voice weakened a bit. "My uncle, you know . . . Ralph. He had given me a pair of regulation cuffs so . . . Anyway we picked the night, but it was cold, really cold." Skate was sweating and his throat was tightening up. "One guy, Ben Groff, he went ahead there, to the farm. The rest of us grabbed Nye. He was easy. Most of the time he was laughing, like he was glad we had picked him. We got him there, and Groff had built a fire so the guy wouldn't freeze. We just . . . handcuffed him to a tree and left. That's all."

"That's all?"

"No, I mean, that's all we did to him. We just left. And we . . . called the president of the pledge class and said we've got Nye, told him approximately where he was. That's all."

Ellen turned to ask him to go on, but her father was so pale and still sweating. He did go on; he took a deep breath and went ahead, shifting in his seat, speaking more quickly now.

"The goddamn bonfire was too big and I guess everything just caught fire, all the trees and brush. We were back to school by then."

"My God, Dad."

"Fire killed the kid."

"*Killed* him?"

"See, the pledges, the goddamn pledges had been so goddamn slow about getting out to that farm. See, Nye was always getting grabbed because he was so easy, because he wanted it, you know. So the pledges just didn't care enough. Oh, it's Nye again. Y' know? Anyway, by the time they got there, the firemen were fighting the fire. Just a small fire; didn't spread much. A fireman found the body."

Ellen was quiet. She had turned to the ocean. She was watching the endless water and thinking about Randal Nye. She understood him, his eagerness, his delight at being pulled into the center of the circle for once. She tried to imagine his last few minutes alive, then she blinked those thoughts away. It was too terrible, *seeing* the fire, *knowing*. And the handcuffs. Ellen found when she spoke that she was crying. "Jesus, Dad . . . the handcuffs." Her father didn't respond. She watched the gray water a while. Then he spoke.

"So now listen, Ellen, Randal Nye's father . . . he's gone crazy. He's going around killing people."

She turned to her father.

"The police called me today."

She put a hand on her father's arm, staring at him, shuddering. "Oh Christ, Dad, I've had a feeling, no really, I've had a feeling something was going to happen. It was connected to you. Something . . . Some danger . . ."

"It's you, Ellen."

"What?"

"This old man, Randal Nye's father, he's going around to the five of us, the five men who grabbed his son that night, and he's coming after our children. He's killed two children already. He's after *you*."

She stared and she shook her head no at that impossible thought.

"He wants to do to our kids what we did to his. He's crazy."

She stared past her father, her eyes lost now in sky as gray as the road, gray as the ocean.

"I've got a friend's place in Laguna. It's arranged. Nobody'll know you're there. Mom is meeting us there. He can't find you there. They'll probably pick him up soon."

Ellen was quiet for a long time, not even seeing the ocean any longer. In her mind she saw fire, heard screams, imagined an old man who was crying, who was full of rage. Now she knew what she was in the center of.

"Ellen, they'll pick him up any day now, before he even gets here."

Frank Skate didn't notice that his daughter was shaking her head. "No," she whispered. "He's coming here."

7

"DAN, will you get away from the window, please." Claire and Daniel King were locked in their third-floor apartment, waiting for Detective Dela to come and tell them how to live through this thing. "Please, Dan!"

"All right, I'm just . . ." Dan King was peering through the drapes, looking down at Damen Avenue, looking for an old man. "Just waiting for the cops."

"They'll buzz the buzzer. Please! He could be out there with a gun!"

"Okay. Okay."

She shook her head, impatient with him. She sat with her legs curled under her, a soft, rounded woman repeating the lines of the curved sofa.

Dan came to her. He was smaller, nimble. He dropped to the floor without effort and sat back against her knees. "I don't like the fact that he's made you nervous. That's what I don't like. He has no right to make my wife nervous."

"You're as nervous as I am."

He liked her fingers on his scalp. He closed his eyes. "I'm not nervous. I'm wary, like a cat."

"Bullshit."

"I thrive on danger. No, really."

"Dan, will you stop kidding! How can you kid?"

"Danger makes me horny."

"Damn it, Dan! Stop!" She drew back on the couch, moved away from him. "I can't listen to any jokes now!" Her voice was ready for crying.

He sighed a deep sigh. "Baby . . . please, let me joke. That's how we're going to get through this thing, laughing."

"I can't laugh."

He sighed again and was silent a while. "Claire . . . you know those joints you had?"

"I still have two in my purse. You want one?"

He shook his head. "No. Leave 'em there. When the cop comes, I'm going to turn you in."

"Damn you!" She hit him on top of the head, but she laughed.

In New York, Ben Groff was speaking to an audience of policemen, firemen, and reporters. Behind him were large charts and maps. He was supposed to be briefing these people on Operation Relocation. Op-Re was the plan for moving the patients of the old Crescent Park Hospital to the site of the new Crescent Park Hospital eight blocks away. Op-Re had taken up most of Ben's life for the past six months. Op-Re was two weeks away. As community relations officer for the hospital, it was Ben's job to make sure that the press, the police, and the fire department knew every detail of Op-Re. But Ben Groff was trembling slightly, and he was saying, "Ladies and gentlemen, I'm going to turn this over to my assistant, Ms. Pegi Stanton. She'll . . . continue this. I'll . . . Excuse me, and I'll be back to answer questions."

He walked quickly out into the hall and closed the door behind him. He just stood there a moment. The door opened and pushed him a bit. He stepped aside for the hospital's chief administrator, Al Meyer. Meyer closed the door and took Groff's arm, walked him a few steps down the hall. "Ben, are you sick? What . . . ?"

"No, I . . . just had some news. About an hour ago. I was going to tell you. I thought I could handle the briefing, but I can't, Mr. Meyer."

"Hey, what news? You're shaking. Tell me."

"My family is in danger, the police think. See I was . . . involved in an accident years ago. And the . . . father of the boy who was killed, he's coming after all those people who were involved. He's coming after us now, after our families."

Meyer stared at him, and Groff thought, He can't

grasp it. It's too big and awful for him to understand. It's too strange, too far away from anything in his experience. But I understand. Groff remembered every moment of the capturing and handcuffing of Randal Nye. He remembered every moment of the funeral, remembered the face of Stephen Nye. He understood.

"A crazy man? My God, Ben. Are the police at home?"

"No. They said to move my family, leave town a while until they pick up this guy. He may not be . . . He might still be in Missouri."

"Leave town?"

"Yes!"

"Now?"

"Yes, Mr. Meyer."

"Won't they protect you?"

"They advised me to leave town. I know it's terrible. Right in the middle of Op-Re."

"Op-Re? To hell with Op-Re. Get your family out of the house."

"They're at my wife's parents' place. I thought I could go on here, but I can't."

"Of course, Ben. Of course. You go to them."

"I have to, Mr. Meyer."

"Of course. Go on. Sure you do."

"Yes." Ben nodded a moment, then turned and left.

Meyer watched him walk away down the hall. He wasn't sure Ben Groff was telling the truth. He figured he was either telling the truth, or he had gone crazy under the pressure of Op-Re. Meyer was sorry for him either way.

84 | GERALD DiPEGO

Groff had been nervous for years, visibly nervous, his head loose and jerky on his neck, his throat catching and swallowing, his eyes afraid. People usually liked him, felt a little sorry for him, figured he had always been that way. Groff's nervousness had begun twenty years ago when he had answered the phone in his fraternity house and heard a pledge say, "Hey, there was a *fire* here! There was a *fire* here where you left him! They just found him! They found his body! There was a *fire* here!" Groff had started that fire, built that comfortable bonfire to keep Randal Nye warm while he waited. "There was a *fire* here!" Groff's fire. He had struck the match and created the flame, and the flame had taken a life.

Groff walked through the hospital corridors, not yet heading for his office, just walking. Twenty years ago he had started a letter to the parents of Randal Nye. He hadn't finished it, never mailed it. He knew the others had each written one, but he couldn't. I'm the one who took the life, he thought. I need to give one back. I need to save a life. Then I'll write that letter and the letter will say, "Dear Mr. and Mrs. Nye. I am Benjamin Groff, one of the five men responsible for the death of your son, Randy. I am writing you now to let you know that I have just saved a life. Someone would have died if it weren't for me. I know this doesn't give you back your son, nor does it release me from the guilt and sorrow I feel, but somehow it seems to balance things just a little." He had never saved a life. He had tried to switch his field from journalism to medicine, but he never made medical school. He never saved a life. He almost wrote the Nyes a letter when his son was born twelve years ago.

But that wouldn't have been right. That letter would have said, you no longer have a son, but now *I* do. No. He had never saved a life and never written the letter and now it was too late. The man was coming after his son, Donald, coming to try and kill Donald. Groff put his trembling hands in his pockets. He walked for half an hour through the corridors of the hospital, passing just outside the rooms where lives were lost and saved every day. He never did go to his office for his suit coat or his pipe. His car keys were in his pocket. He fled out the front door.

———————————

Lou Pennamen was head of Dela's homicide squad. He sat on the edge of his chair, watching Dela pacing in front of him, moving around the office with all that energy. He didn't like Dela's energy. He was afraid of it. He was afraid that Dela, only thirty-three, was showing him up, trampling him under all that energy, coming after his job.

"Because, Lou, listen, if we tell King to get out of town or move or change his patterns, we're only delaying things."

"Right. Delaying things till we can pick up this nut if he's here at all."

"But Nye's got all the time in the world. He could cool off in . . . Denver, say, for six months, then come back after King, or after one of the others. If he sees that King has been warned, he could find a hole someplace and just sit tight. He's got money. He's got his savings, fourteen grand." He came closer to Pennamen. "But if we don't change a thing, if we let King move around normally, we'll bring Nye out of his hole. He'll try his hit, and we'll grab him once and for all."

"You'd be taking a chance."

"I'll leave it up to King. I think any of these guys would rather see Nye caught than live with this over their heads. Remember, Nye is no professional. He's clumsy, renting a car in his own name and running over that kid. He'll try to contact King or he'll make some clumsy try at him, and we'll get the bastard."

"You don't even know if Nye is in town."

"I'm sure he'll come here next."

"Dela, you're not sure of anything! Maybe he only wanted to kill two of them. Anyway, King doesn't even *have* a kid!"

"So this time he'll go right for the man, for King. It makes it easier for us."

"No. Look, you prove to me that Nye is in Chicago or near Chicago, and you can play it that way for a while. Otherwise, don't put any hours into this."

Dela circulated a current photo of Nye all over the city and suburbs. He spoke to the police in Iverson about their search of Nye's home and their interviews with his friends. He asked the police in Rockford, Illinois, to locate and question the former Elaine Nye, who was remarried and believed to be living in their city. He went to see Mr. and Mrs. Daniel King.

Dela was cool when he called on the Kings. The intensity was held back, only visible behind his eyes. He spoke softly, moved in small, smooth motions, sitting on their couch, opening his suit coat. The Kings kept glancing at his chest, his belt, wondering where his gun was. It was in his raincoat pocket, and the coat was hanging, dripping over their bathtub. His hair was wet, but it didn't seem to bother him, and he said no to both coffee and a drink. They had expected two cops, or at least one older cop, or at least a bigger cop. But in listening to Dela and watching him move and searching his eyes, they found comfort. He knew what he was doing, and what he was doing was important to him.

"What do you remember about Stephen Nye?"

"I only remember him at the funeral, staring at me."

"Did he say anything to you or the other four?"

"I don't think he said anything to anybody."

"Mr. . . . . Dela?" Claire King made a question of his name.

"Jim," Dela said, but she didn't use the name.

"Since we don't have any children, don't you think he'll leave us alone?"

"What do *you* think, Mr. King?" Dela watched them ponder that, uncomfortable with it. He liked these two. He liked the way the woman sat so close to her husband, touching him with her leg and hip and shoulder. Dan King was a slight man with small hands and feet. Dela thought maybe he had been a dancer. Claire King was attractively ample. She seemed to lean against her husband now out of a need to keep in contact, to keep him safe. "He's out for revenge," Dela said. "He's gotten to two out of the five of you. You think he'll stop?"

Dan thought a moment more, then shook his head. "He's a big man. Pretty old now, I guess."

"Sixty-three."

"But a big guy, and I remember him staring right at

me, right at . . . all five of us. I thought he might just run over and start swinging at us. I remember thinking that. So now he did. He just waited twenty years. Now he's running at us and swinging. I think you'll have to catch him."

Dela nodded. "I will catch him."

Claire said, "I'm glad you're so *sure*."

Dela leaned forward. Her words had thrown a spark into his eyes. "I'm a slow reader, Mrs. King." They waited for more words, afraid he was mad at them. "And I hate writing—even reports. Nye is an English teacher, and he's great at that stuff. But now he's taking up something new. He's into a whole new world. Homicide. *My* world." Dela paused a moment and sat back. "The old son of a bitch is an amateur." Dela grinned the faintest of grins, and the Kings visibly relaxed.

Late that afternoon a Rockford, Illinois, detective named Karis came to the house of Elaine Glorfeld, the former Mrs. Nye. She was a widow, living alone, sixty years old. Karis had called her, so when he came to the door, she was expecting him.

"Please come in . . . sit down."

"Thanks."

"You say it concerns my ex-husband?"

"Stephen Nye. Have you heard from him recently?"

"Stephen? Not for nearly twenty years. Why?"

They took seats facing each other in the living room, a very pretty room, full of plants and lovely things placed carefully on polished wooden tables and shelves. Elaine was lovely too, grown stately and white-haired. She sat gracefully, her head tilted with her question, her intelligent eyes narrowed a bit, waiting for the answer.

Karis leaned forward and told her the facts that had come to him from Missouri via Chicago. He told her about Bob Davis spinning down through the dark to an alley floor and about Tom Johns being smashed to death by the front of a car.

Elaine's head straightened slowly as the man talked, and her eyes widened and then filled with tears and then closed. She sat back in her chair and covered her face.

"Should I stop, Mrs. Glorfeld?"

She shook her head, and he went on, cautioning her, asking her to notify him if her ex-husband contacted her, asking her for any insights into Stephen's personality.

She was silent a long while, her hands still to her face. "I'd like to be alone." The words were soft. She didn't look at him. "I'll call you . . . if I hear anything, and I'll . . . be able to talk more to you tomorrow."

"All right, Mrs. Glorfeld."

After Karis left, she slowly brought her hands down into her lap. She leaned her head against the back of the chair and sobbed freely for a long time, soft sounds that filled up the dim and pretty room as the last of the window light faded and darkness came.

Every time Dela approached the door to his apartment, he had the feeling that someone was waiting inside, an enemy waiting to pounce or stab or shoot.

He walked on toward his door, his steps silent on

the hallway carpet. There was no sound except the nonsound that was the building's life system, a constant whispering hum. It was a new building, the air centrally heated and cooled, the lights on timers, the elevators quiet and automatic. Dela heard nothing, saw only his door looming larger as he neared it. When he opened the door, it would be dark in there, and in the dark could be a cop killer, or an ex-con come to settle a score, or a friend of a man Dela had put away, or maybe all three plus some tough youths he had rousted and a junkie he had collared.

He inserted the key, feeling the presence of at least fifteen assassins behind the door. The feeling came more from movies than from his life, came from watching those scenes where the detective enters his room and is attacked in the dark.

Dela unlocked the door and withdrew his key, pushed the door open ahead of him, walking in fast and thinking, Fuck you, assholes. Dela always met fear with anger, charging instead of retreating, going in with his chin and chest stuck out and his arms tight and ready. He had always met fear that way, even as a little boy with tears in his eyes and his heart pounding. He had lunged forward, mad as hell. It was his way of being afraid.

He slapped at a light switch, walking in, and his moment of anger left with the darkness. He went into the bathroom to hang up his wet raincoat and came out rubbing a towel on his black curly hair.

He lived in a furnished, one-room apartment with his bed folded up now into a couch. It was neat and very modern and a little too expensive for him. The building was a high-rise near the lake.

He liked the peace and order of his apartment, all

the neat right angles, the reflections in chrome and glass. He was proud of this place, but not really at home in it. Someone else had chosen these things and bought them and arranged them. If Dela had had to do it, he wouldn't have known how. Whenever he had a friend over from the squad or brought a woman here, he was vaguely anxious about the things that filled his room. They were lies. They weren't him.

He turned the volume all the way down on his TV set, then clicked it on, wanting only the colored images in his room now, not the voices. He rubbed his hair dry, watching a commercial. He moved to his stereo set and punched a button for FM radio. The music was soft. It was there if he cared to listen, like the silent images on the TV screen, there if he cared to watch.

Dela had lived in stark rooms of stark, hollow houses that were never filled-in by enough people or furniture or quiet talk or laughter. These were places to leave early in the morning and come back to for sleep. He had spent his days in schools and on the streets, and the streets were no home either. He had learned to survive them, to walk them unafraid, but they didn't belong to him any more than this apartment did. He was a stationary transient. His clothes hung in closets and lay folded in drawers. His name was on the door and on the lease, but even when he was in, he wasn't home.

He took a half-full bottle of wine from the refrigerator and poured a glass. He opened a book to a marked page. The book was *The Book of Wines*, and he read again the description of the wine he was sipping. Dela felt he should know wines, not to impress people, but for himself. He could pronounce the French names very well, but he almost never did. He would point to a name on a wine list or mumble it or even fracture it on purpose, too self-conscious to say it right. He hated himself at times like that.

At times like that, he would hear a signal in his mind, a siren, a warning. Don't make a fool of yourself, it would say. He would be about to order wine. He would be about to lift his little nephew to his breast. He would be about to expose his soul. Don't be a fool, the signal would caution, and Dela would pull back, away from the edge, to stand on safe, familiar ground.

He sipped the wine and took it with him to the window. All the images were there. Dela's apartment was reflected in the glass, and beyond the glass were Dela's streets. He sat and watched the rain, watched the reflected television picture, watched himself sipping wine. Only the rain was real.

8

S TEPHEN NYE sat up in bed, sweating and shivering, his arms stretching out in front of him. He closed his eyes and held his breath until he could feel the tiny key in his right hand, until he could feel and see that key slip into the lock and loosen the cuffs and free his son. His breath came now in a great sob as he imagined holding his son and running with him out of the flames, away from death, into the cool dark forest that was still alive.

He brought his knees up and rested his head on them. His hands were fists, pressing on his temples. He wept freely.

Stephen realized that that one act was what he wanted more than anything, that act of saving his son, that moment that had never happened, that charge through the flames to that screaming helpless child, that quick, sure unlocking, that strong wonderful swoop of his arms that brought the child up off the ground, that joyous, tearful run with the child crying against his chest, with both of them crying as they left the roaring, crackling death behind them.

His tears ended in long, shuddering breaths, and he became aware of the rain whipping against his window in windblown splatters. He rose and went to the storm, watched it a long time. It soothed him. It turned the fire in his mind to smoke and pelted the ashes until even the smoke was gone.

"Dad?"

Stephen turned to see Randy seated on the bed, but it was Randy's bed in Randy's room now. The boy was sixteen. He had stopped wearing pajamas, went to bed in undershirt and briefs. Stephen stepped into the boy's room. "Thought you were asleep, Rand."

"I keep thinking about what you said. About Gloria."

He sat on the bed next to his son. "What about her?"

"We're not going steady or engaged or anything."

"I know, I just . . ."

"We haven't planned a future or anything. Geez, our future is . . . it seems a million days away. Just school, college, we talk about that. I talk about history and she's interested in teaching little kids. We want to travel a lot. I know I'm going to Africa; I just *know* that. But not necessarily with Gloria."

"I was just surprised, Rand, when you said 'girlfriend.' I knew she was your friend."

"She's my friend and she's a girl, that's all."

Stephen shook his head and stared off, felt his son watching him and waiting for his words. "No, when you say 'girlfriend,' it means something more than friend. Maybe you don't realize it yet. That's why I got a little upset, Rand. Girlfriend. I suddenly pictured you and Gloria walking down the aisle." Randy laughed and bounced on the bed a bit. Stephen smiled, going on. "I got worried that you were making commitments. Friendship is fine, but you have to stand back a bit from those emotional commitments, stand back until everybody is ready. Does she call you her boyfriend?"

"Well . . ." Randy shrugged, then nodded.

"See that's what concerns me, Rand. Here's somebody who feels she's . . . attached to you and you to her. I don't like to think of you with any attachments on you. You don't owe . . . . You owe your love and your loyalties only within the family. The rest comes later. Later, okay?"

"Daddy?"

Stephen turned to see Randy, at seven, standing in the doorway. Elaine stirred in the bed beside Stephen. Stephen whispered, "Randy, what's wrong?"

"I had a nightmare and I have to go to the bathroom."

Stephen rose, still whispering. "C'mon let's not bother Mom. I'll stay in your room a while. What did you dream about?"

"The house exploded."

He picked up the boy, walking to the bathroom. "What else?"

"I flew up and hit birds in the sky."

"Hold on," Stephen said. "If the place explodes, we go up together, okay?"

Ellen lay on a bed in a little boy's room. The house belonged to a friend of her father's. They must have a boy about five or six or seven, she guessed. Maybe a girl, but she didn't think so—all soldiers and trucks and planes in the room. A broken helmet. A plastic machine gun. The bed was small, but not too small if she didn't sprawl in it. Ellen usually slept as if she had fallen on the bed from some great height, arms spread, a knee hiked up. Now she lay straight and still, her clothes on, even her sandals. She listened to the ocean and to the voice of the house.

It was the same voice she had heard in the house in San Francisco where she grew from zero to eleven. It was the combined sounds of her parents arguing in some distant room. It was a murmur with an edge to it. It was a sad and angry voice.

Ellen closed her eyes and tried to make the sound of the ocean erase the voice of the house. It couldn't. She turned out the light and went to her window, pulled the curtains aside, opened the window. It was dark, but the moon showed her the waves and the white surf, and the wind brought her the ocean's loud breathing. The voice of the house was drowned and all her memories of San Francisco swept away. She looked at the waves and thought about all the people who were thinking about her.

She was on the list on the desk of at least five

policemen—one in each city. She was on the minds of the other intended victims and their families. She was on the list of a murderer. Maybe he was looking at her name right now. Or her photo—maybe he had pictures of her. Or maybe he was looking at *her*. Maybe he was on the deck of a boat out on that dark water, looking at her through the scope of a rifle. Bam. She imagined it. Would she know what had happened? Or would the hole appear in the glass and the gun go off and the bullet strike her and her life end all in the same second? She didn't move from the window. She stared deep into the darkness, watching for a boat.

The door to her room opened and she jumped, gasped, turned. "Jesus Christ, Mom! Knock!"

"Ellen, come here," her mother said, already walking away.

They assembled in the living room. It felt like San Francisco again.

"Are we going to have an argument for old times' sake?" Ellen said. "Just to make this gathering official."

Her mother's eyes looked hurt, but her mouth was thin and mean and ready to bite. "What in God's name were you doing when your father picked you up?"

Ellen turned to her father. "Why did you tell her that? I explained. Dad? I explained to you."

"What were you doing?! Your father is blaming me and I want to know!"

Ellen stepped close to him, nearly in tears. "Why did you tell her?"

"It's just one more thing," Frank said. "Something else to worry about. Jesus *Christ*! I'm sick of it."

"He said you were naked!"

"I was dancing."

"Dancing! Flying high on some kind of dope or drink or what?"

"Dancing!"

"The three of you—you and Ann and a man together naked—what kind of sickness is that?"

Ellen turned to her. "You've been naked! Your clothes aren't sewn on. Jesus!"

"Is this what we're paying for?" Her mother advanced on her. "Is this why we're letting you have a place of your own? So you can cheapen yourself? So you can have lovers!"

"No," Ellen said quietly. "So *you* can."

Her mother slapped her. Ellen saw it coming and took it mostly on her hand, but the tears came anyway. "Dad, give her your belt. Let's do this right."

Frank pounded a fist on the bar top, once, twice. The glasses and bottles danced in circles. "Look at you two! Every time I see you, I walk into a goddamn ambush. The two of you are laying for me with another goddamn crisis. You dig pits for me! First you get her out of the house and turn her loose in Los Angeles . . ."

"Don't throw it all on me," her mother said. "She never listens to me."

He pointed at Ellen. "And *you*—for God's sake . . ."

"What? Me what, Dad?"

"You've decided to do anything you can to make me worry about you so that you . . . stick in my brain, and I can't have a minute! You can't just go to school and grow up and . . . . You go crazy and turn yourself loose and make yourself easy!"

Ellen ran for the door.

"Don't you leave here!" her mother said. But Ellen was out on the low balcony now, and jumping over its railing, landing on the sand below, and running to the beach. She heard her parents shouting from the balcony.

"Ellen!"

"Don't go out there!"

"Ellen he could be out there!"

She stopped at the water's edge, let the foam wash up on her sandals, up to her ankles. In a moment she heard her parents coming across the sand. Her mother was crying now. "Go inside, Ellen, please. We're all so nervous over this thing. My God. Your father drives me *crazy* with this thing, this crazy murderer. I'm half insane!" Her mother turned and struck out at her father. "Why did you have to do that to that boy! You and your stupid friends!"

"Go inside, Ellen, and stay there." Her father sounded tough, but he wouldn't drag her back there. He wouldn't let himself get wet and sandy. There was no way that they could make her go back in there. She walked a little farther out into the water.

"Ellen."

Her mother screamed and wept. "Ellen, what if that man is out here!"

She walked away from her parents, moving along the edge of the surf. She took her sandals off and went to where the water washed at her knees, and the waves pulled the sand from under her feet. Her parents stood about fifty feet away, watching her, calling to her from time to time, arguing in a murmur that rose and fell under the sound of the surf.

Ellen watched the waves come and cover her knees, retreat again. Then she looked far out to sea, looking for a boat, waiting for a rifle shot. Would she see the flame from the gun, she wondered. Or would the flame and the shot and her death happen all together?

9

THURSDAY morning. Daniel King called his boss and said he had the flu. He'd be back to work Monday. He had been instructed to do this by Detective Dela. Dela had no approval to stake out the Kings' apartment, to assign himself or others to protect King. So he gambled. He felt if he kept the Kings safely locked in their apartment, Thursday through Sunday, it would give him enough time to find some trace of Stephen Nye. All he needed was a trace, some bit of evidence that Nye was in Chicago. Then Dela could get the approval for the full-time operation he wanted, for the stakeout, for the trap.

Thursday evening. Dela called on the Kings on his way home. He pressed the downstairs buzzer, and Claire King's voice came over the intercom with a nervous edge to it. "Who is it?"

Dela answered, and she buzzed down, unlocking the door to the lobby. Dela hesitated, staring at the fifty names, the fifty white buttons on the tenant list. He let the lobby door close, let it lock him once more in the foyer. Then he slowly moved his finger down a row of buttons, pressing each one, buzzing ten apartments. Several voices questioned him on the intercom, but someone simply buzzed back, opening the door, letting him into the building.

He shook his head, walking to the elevator. When he arrived at the Kings' apartment, he told them, "Don't rely on the buzzer system to keep him out of the building. If somebody knocks on your door, you be absolutely sure who it is before you make a move. Talk through the door, and don't go right for the peephole. If it's Nye, the bastard could knock and then just shoot through the door. You be sure."

Claire shuddered and took her husband's hand.

"You two need anything from outside?"

"Some good news," Dan said.

"Nye's photo is being circulated to everybody with a hotel, motel, room for rent—everybody in a ten-block circle around this place and around your office. Just sit tight; stay away from the windows and the door."

"Can we have people over?" Claire said. "A couple of friends? Anybody?"

"Sure, just be careful when they're coming in. And

don't talk about this. If it becomes big news, then Nye'll hear about it and get scared off."

"Is that bad?" she said.

Dela looked at her a while, then at Dan. "You want to be wondering about this guy for months or *years*? It's really up to you. You could go hide somewhere. You could move to a different town. . . ."

"No," Dan said. "We'll do it like we said, but hurry up and get the guy, will you? I can't last much longer trapped in here with a woman who won't keep her hands off me."

Claire hit her husband's shoulder. It was part of their act, an unconscious routine. He did the jokes; she reacted; the audience laughed. Dela was not a good audience. He nodded and went out the door. They locked and chained it after him.

Friday morning. Dan and Claire slept late and had a long, lazy breakfast. They didn't speak about Nye or Dela. They enjoyed each other. They spoke of the finest moments, the funniest moments of their two-year-old marriage. They laughed until tears came. They made love. They stepped into their tub to shower together and turned the water on and then suddenly stared at each other, realizing at the same moment that, beneath the morning's talk and laughter and lust, both of them had been listening hard for the phone to ring—so hard that its *not* ringing had become a sound, a steady unbroken hum. They couldn't shower together because what if it rang and they didn't hear it? What if it was a call to give them the news that it was all over, or a call to warn them? Claire stepped out of the shower and put her robe on, sat in the bedroom staring at her thoughts and listening to the phone not ringing.

Friday night. The Kings were preparing for the arrival of their friends, the Natelys. They were good enough friends so that they didn't need to be polite. They could say terrible things to each other for fun, just to make everyone laugh, and they *would* laugh. The Kings needed to laugh and forget.

Claire had pulled her light brown hair back into a bun, but it was unraveling already, wispy strands alive in the lamplight. Her hands were not efficient tonight, and she was smoking too much, eating too much. Dan's nerves made him restless. He had fixed everything in the apartment that was broken or even threatening to break.

The Natelys were due at eight, and by seven-thirty the drinks were all but mixed, the snacks were out, the Kings were dressed and ready and promising each other that they wouldn't even hint to the Natelys about what they were going through. They were eager for guests. They were excited, even giddy.

It was the door buzzer that punctured their mood. They remembered what Dela had said. When the Natelys knocked on their door, Claire and Dan looked at each other for a moment before Dan moved to let them in.

"Dan. . . ." She couldn't help saying it. "Check first."

Dan turned to her and nodded, spoke through the door. "Who is it?"

"It's us, for God's sake. What's this 'Who is it'?"

Dan opened the door and the Natelys came in laughing. They were a bit younger than the Kings and very hearty, booming with cheer. They soon filled the room with voices raised in greetings and teasing and jokes private to the four of them. But they didn't laugh for long. By the middle of the first drink they had the scent of trouble. There were gaps, hushes, forced talk. Nate said, "Hey, you guys. What's wrong?"

Dan and Claire looked at each other. They sighed. They smiled a bit, knowing they had to tell, they both *wanted* to tell. They told—everything from Randal Nye to Stephen Nye to Dela. It was the most exciting thing the Natelys had ever been told. It was the most interesting evening the two couples had ever shared. The story changed every window in the apartment into a place of possible danger, and it made the door an electric, vibrating threat. What if he were out there? They even turned out the lights and peered through the windows. He's tall. Here's his picture. Could *that* be . . . ? No. Look! Is that . . . ? No, silly. They laughed. They worried. The Natelys stared at the Kings with awe, shook their heads and said, "Jesus" or "Wow," again and again. The Kings nodded, smiled, held hands. They talked until 2 A.M. The Natelys were afraid to leave. They snuck out like spies. The Kings watched them from the edge of their window, all the lights out. No one slept until dawn.

Saturday afternoon. Patrolman Jesse Stacey got a positive identification of Stephen Nye's photo from L. Ted Jones, manager of the Clarendon Hotel, two and a half blocks from the Kings' apartment. Mr. Jones identified the photo as the man in Number Eleven.

The name on the register was James Joyce. He had checked in six days ago.

Patrolman Stacey radioed for assistance, and when that assistance arrived, he and his partner went to Room Eleven and found it locked. They had Mr. Jones open the door. Stephen Nye, alias James Joyce, was not there, but his belongings were. At that moment detectives Dela and Bridger arrived. It was 1:18 P.M.

Dela ordered the uniformed patrolmen out of the area, angry that they had been so visible in the hotel. He placed Bridger in Mr. Jones's office with Mr. Jones. They could see the lobby from an office window. Dela remained in Room Eleven. A second team of detectives arrived and were placed in back of and across the street from the hotel.

Dela sat on Stephen Nye's bed and moved his eyes slowly around the room. He saw things he wanted to examine, papers he wanted to study, but he sat still. Stephen Nye lived in this room, and the room was alive with his presence. Dela didn't want to destroy that. He didn't want to go moving about in a rush, disturbing things, making noise, driving away the aura of Stephen Nye. It was Dela's way to be still a while, hold his energy and emotions back a while, let the room alone, let it live around him. He waited until he began to hear the floor and walls creaking here and there, began to hear the water dripping in the sink, began to feel invisible. Now he could move about carefully and quietly inside Nye's room, inside Nye's skull, looking with Nye's eyes and hearing with his ears, hoping for clues that would give him passage into Nye's mind, windows to his thoughts. This was the way Dela worked and why he loved his work. When he set out to catch someone, he *became* that someone, became him as deeply, as hard as he could. Burrowed into his mind. Lived in his mind. *Knew* him.

He was beginning to know Stephen Nye, just beginning.

Nye had nearly fourteen thousand in savings, yet he had chosen a cheap hotel. There were better ones in the area, but this one was more anonymous. That was smart. No one really saw the people who lived in hotels like this. They were usually old and poor and sick and alone and transparent. Nobody looked *at* them. They were people made of glass and Nye could disappear among them.

The suitcase was new, large and black and average. The toilet articles were long-used, part of a routine carried over from the old life to the new. Some new clothes, cheap and plain. Five folders containing information on the five men who had been responsible for the death of his son. Most of the information was typed, some notes were in longhand, a neat, readable hand, sure and simple.

While Dela searched, part of his mind waited for the one half-ring of the phone that was Bridger's signal that Nye was on his way up. After a few minutes, the revolver in Dela's pocket seemed to be getting heavier. He was becoming more and more aware of its weight, and his right hand was tingling a bit, the fingers ready to grasp the handle of the gun, to hold the familiar shape and find the safety and the trigger. When Nye came through that door, it would all be over in a quick movement of Dela's hands—one hand for his detective's shield, one for his gun, pointing them at Nye, stopping him, turning him to stone. It would be over, and Dela would be calling Dan King saying, This is Dela. We got him. He imagined that, said it inside his mind. We got him.

The phone rang. It wasn't the signal from Bridger. It was a full ring, then another. Someone was calling Room Eleven from outside. Dela hesitated.

Stephen Nye stood among the magazine racks of a large drugstore on Damen Avenue and peered through the one uncluttered portion of store window, staring across the street and down four buildings toward the apartment of Daniel King. For the past several days he had spent hours in the drugstore, glancing through magazines, staring through that window, eating at the drugstore fountain, going back to the window, buying books and magazines so that the store manager would think of him as a customer and not just an old man who came in to look through the magazines. He even bought a watch for forty dollars, a key chain, and three pairs of socks.

Unless he kept missing them, the Kings were not coming out of their apartment. He knew that Daniel King had not been to work Thursday and Friday. He also knew that their car was in the building's parking lot. But since Thursday he had not seen the Kings and he *had* seen twice as many police cars cruising in the area.

Fear warred with the feeling of power inside of

him. The two emotions struck him in waves. He would review the death of Bob Davis in his mind, and the death of Thomas Johns, and he would feel as sure as fate itself. His acts were part of the order of the universe, locked in place. Somewhere in the future he had already punished Daniel King and Stephen Groff and Frank Skate. It was done. It was begun. He could not be stopped. Then the feeling of power would wash away as a wave of fear engulfed him. There are policemen searching for *me*, he would think, for Stephen Nye, whose quiet, passive life had never brushed with violence, never encountered real enemies, never stimulated real anger in anyone. Me. People are hating and hunting *me*. At those moments he would want to run, and perhaps he might have weakened and fled if he had had any place to go. He had no place, no people, no life, no reason for being except his plan. He had nowhere to go except to march along that red line he had drawn across the country, making five stops.

Another police car cruised past the store window, and Stephen knew he must change, change his name again, change his face, his walk, erase the man they were looking for, replace him. He had already begun to change. He had bought eyeglasses, though his vision was nearly perfect. He had let his hair grow longer. He had bought hair dye and even looked at wigs and false mustaches, but all of these things made the fear rise again in waves that weakened him, panicked him. Me! They're hunting me! How can I change? How can I hide? He remembered playing hiding games as a child. He could find the darkest corners and squeeze far back into the shadows, but when the hunter had come near, he had almost always surrendered. He hadn't had the courage to stay hidden and hold his breath and really test himself against that hunter. Now he had to.

He stiffened as he saw someone coming out of the King's building. It wasn't them, but it was an older couple he recognized. When he first arrived, he had seen the Kings leave the building with this couple. They had all gone food shopping together, and Nye had followed them. He had filled a cart with groceries as he moved with them through the aisles of the store, studying Dan King, putting his image together with the photos in his folder, with his memories of the funeral. Dan had been the smallest, a slight boy, blond. He had wept at the gravesite. He and Benjamin Groff had truly sobbed, and Groff had suddenly sat down on the grass, put his head in his hands. Dan King had comforted him. Stephen remembered this as he studied King and studied his wife. They liked each other; they joked, once they even kissed quickly and laughed as he watched them. The other couple was older, next-door neighbors Stephen guessed. Two tall, stooped, sagging people. They walked back to the building with the Kings, both couples wheeling their groceries in little carts, like parents with strollers, chatting as they walked. Nye had walked with them, across the street from them, watching.

Now he left the drugstore. He followed the older couple as they went to the food store. He stayed close to them, pretending to shop, listening to them and hoping they would mention the Kings, but they didn't.

Stephen walked back to his hotel. A thought he'd

had before came thrusting at him—that he was found out, that he was trapped, but he pushed it away, erased it for a while by remembering an argument he had had with his son. He played it out in his mind, and it made him walk more quickly toward his hotel, toward Room Eleven, where James Dela waited.

"Do you see what's happened?" He was shouting at Randy. "Can you hear yourself? Every other sentence has that fraternity in it. The Sigma Delta house, the Sigma Delta actives, the Sigma Delta pledges . . ."

"What's wrong with my talking about it? I'm *in* the pledge class so I talk about it!"

"You're starting to narrow yourself down. I can tell!" Stephen made fists and waved them in front of his own face, straining to be understood, straining to convince. They were sitting in his parked car. He had just visited Randy at his dorm. He had met some of his Sigma Delta friends. "You're starting to narrow the world down, and I want it to be wide open to you! And I want you to be completely free in that world!"

"I will be, Dad." Randy was near tears.

"Not hammered into a routine like I was, hammered to fit into a neat little passageway that led me through organized schoolwork, right to a nice little job teaching more organized schoolwork to students who don't care because they're just . . . traveling along their own little passageways. And they never question it! And I never questioned it. But *you*!"

"I'll be free, Dad."

"You'll have a wide-open education, and then our trip, Rand. I've been saving . . ."

"I know, Dad. I think about our trip all the time." The boy was crying a little now.

"You'll see the world and study it and be able to choose. When I think of being with you in all those places . . ."

"That hasn't changed, Dad."

"It changes every time you say Sigma Delta. It sounds like a hammer to me, hammer blows shaping you into something—too soon! Too soon!"

"They're just my friends, Dad. I *want* friends. I want to . . ." The boy's tears overwhelmed his speech, and someone said "Hello there . . ."

Stephen stopped his quick walk, his heart caught. He turned toward the voice.

"Hello there, you're on my floor."

Stephen glanced at the man, and then actually glanced down at the sidewalk, bewildered. "Your floor?"

"At the hotel." The man was not old really, younger than Stephen, but spent, shrunken. He had no teeth, wore a shapeless blob of a coat. Stephen had seen him at the hotel several times, but had never really looked at him.

"Oh, at the hotel."

"Yeah, at the Clarendon." The man smiled. "I stay here most of the time."

"Here?"

"Here." The man gestured toward a shop window. It was a laundromat. Stephen could hear some of the washers hissing, the rumble and groaning of machinery. "Don't like the crowd at the Clarendon. Sit in the lobby and talk dirt about the people that don't show up. I've heard 'em. I come here. There's chairs."

Stephen nodded at the man, who was beginning to disappear. He was thinking of other things now.

"Vending machines. I read here. People come in, out. Plenty of talk."

"Nice to see you," Stephen said, smiling vaguely in the direction of the voice, turning away.

"Clean in here."

Stephen nodded, walking away. He heard the man take a few steps after him.

"They got a coffee machine. Want some?"

Stephen half turned. "No, thanks."

"Police at the hotel."

"What?" The man became solid again, smiling at Stephen, the smile wrinkling his face like an old brown bag.

"Yeah, police at the Clarendon today. Guys in the lobby said, 'Hey, what're the police doin' up there?' I just walk through. I don't talk to them. I come here."

Stephen brushed past the man and walked quickly into the laundry, stood there stiff and panicked. The man came in.

"Want some? Coffee?"

Stephen didn't look at him, didn't move at all. Me! They're hunting me! Move! Hide! "Phone in here?" His voice was shaky. The man pointed to a battered pay phone on the wall and Stephen turned to it. He fumbled with the phonebook, realizing the man was close to him, watching him, wondering. He tried a smile to put the man at ease. His lips trembled. He found the number, threw a quarter in the phone because it was the first coin he found. He called for a Yellow Cab and told the man to send it to the laundromat on Damen near Clarendon. "What's the name of this place? The address!"

The man looked at him wide-eyed, then he did a

strange shuffling run outside to read the number and the same run back to Stephen. He called out the address importantly and proudly.

Stephen hung up and tried to catch his breath. He sat, already watching out the window for the cab. Then he stood and moved to a chair deeper inside the building. The man watched him all the while, baffled and excited. He came over to Stephen and asked him again if he wanted coffee. Stephen stared at the window and didn't answer. The man sat next to him, watching him.

Stephen was that little boy again, playing hide-and-go-seek, squeezed far back into the shadows. The hunter was very close, coming closer.

A clothes dryer was banged open and Stephen jumped, turned on a woman who was busy folding her clothes. His mouth was dry and his hand trembled and he was ashamed. Where was the power? Had he dreamed it, or had he really killed two people, caused two of those five men to suffer. He *had* done it. He *had* the power. He looked at his trembling hands, and he heard himself sob, a small shaky sob. He tightened his hands. How could they stop him? He was a father charging through the flames to save his son. How could they stop him?

Stephen's hands were reaching out in front of him, his arms stiff. The man next to him was staring open-mouthed. The woman folding her clothes stopped to gaze at him.

How could they stop him? It was Randy he was avenging. Randy. They had bound that boy and burned him. Randy, who wanted to laugh. He saw Randy in the park, sitting on the ground in a crowd of kids, watching a puppet show. The puppets did something funny, and Randy turned to the strangers around him, children he didn't know, and he laughed, wanting to laugh *with* them, to join them. The other children only looked straight ahead, didn't see him. Stephen, sitting far back with the parents, saw that and felt his throat fill with crying. I'll laugh with you, Rand, he thought. I'll always laugh with you.

Stephen suddenly rose out of his chair, filled with a fury. He hurried back to the pay phone. The man shuffled after him. Stephen found a dime and turned to the man, his eyes fierce. The man took a step back. "What's the hotel's number?" Stephen said. "The phone number!"

Dela decided to answer the phone ringing in Number Eleven. He picked it up after five rings. " 'Lo."

"I know this is a policeman."

"Who is this?"

"Stephen Nye."

"Shit!" Dela had guessed wrong. He should've let it ring. The bastard was better at this than Dela thought, or he had been warned. Now he would *not* be walking through that door; now it was a whole new game.

"Nye, what the fuck do you think you're doing? You think we let people wander around killing children? I'm telling you here and now it's over. Where are you?"

"I just called to say I'm not running away. I'm staying."

"Staying where?"

"I'm staying here in this city until it's done."

"It's over, Nye. You made your point. You avenged your son. You killed two boys, so now it's over, and you come and tell me all about it. It's important that I hear *your* side now, and I'll give you my name and you pick the place. We'll talk, and you'll have a chance to tell your side of the story." He didn't know if Nye was completely crazy. He didn't know if Bridger was tracing the call through the switchboard downstairs. He just kept talking. "My name is James Dela. I'll meet you anywhere you say, just to talk."

"I'm saying goodbye now, Mr. Dela. We'll never meet. I'm going to New York when I'm finished here."

"Listen, asshole, you come anywhere near Dan King, and I'll climb all over you, you fucking psycho. Who do you think you are? You think a bunch of people have to die just because you say so?"

"Goodbye, Mr. Del . . ."

"Wait a minute! Hey! About that boy of yours, about that son. I hear he was a fag." Silence now. He had gripped him with that, held Nye on the other end of the wire a few more precious seconds. "I've been talking to the guys that knew him. They say he was a pervert. Is that true?"

"You bastard."

"Did he take after you, you crazy asshole? Hey, hey, Nye, I'll meet you anywhere you say, just me and you. I'll tell you all about your son."

"I'm coming, Dela, but you won't see me. I'm coming after Dan King."

"Not in my town! Hey!" Dela was shouting into the phone as he heard Nye hang up. "Hey! *Not in my town, you old fart!*" He was disconnected. He raised the receiver like a club and brought it down hard on the telephone table. "Asshole!" He threw the receiver into its cradle and waited. The phone rang, and he snatched it up. It was Bridger.

"Yeah?"

"We didn't get it, Del."

"Shit. All right, listen." He sat on the bed. "Call Mortimer. We're going to talk to every resident, everybody around here. We're going to pack up every thread in this room and take it with us. Did you listen to this asshole?"

"Yeah. He means it, buddy."

"He's a fucking teacher, an amateur."

"He means it."

Dela hung up and looked around him. All right, he thought, it's a new game. He knows we're ready for him; and he's still coming. All right. Dela listened until his mind cleared and he could hear the sink dripping again. Everything in this room would help him learn about Stephen Nye, help him crawl inside the man, *be* the man. He went to work.

10

Ellen made a ring of furniture along the walls of the room so she could dance in the middle. She had found a small phonograph and a stack of children's records in the cabinet. She danced to the themes from Disney movies, danced and clowned for an imaginary audience of kids seated around her on the empty chairs, empty bed. She changed characters, improvising a Mary Poppins dance, Baloo the Bear dance, Fairy Godmother dance. She made funny faces and even added pratfalls and looks of great surprise. The kids loved it.

All the while the surf was attacking the shore just fifty feet from her window. Whenever she looked at it, she felt small and dumb, dancing alone in a room when all that was going on just fifty feet away, all that chaos of rocks and foam and sand.

Her mother opened the door and leaned in, excited. "He's for sure in Chicago," her mother said. "They've seen him there."

Ellen turned off the phonograph. "Oh. They've seen him?" That made Stephen Nye a solid, real man. Someone had seen him. He was not a giant, shadow-black threat, blowing toward California like a storm. He must be a man with a body and limbs and a regular head because someone, after all, had seen him.

"The police called your father. They almost caught him! They're very close! God. At least we can breathe now."

"We can go to the beach." She moved past her mother. "Come on."

"I'm not dressed for the beach."

"Just come out, Mom. I want to show you something." Ellen was running out the door. "Come on!"

She ran down to the wet sand, glad to be so close a witness to the important meeting of the ocean and the beach. She watched the event take place. The rocks seemed dashed and destroyed, but they rose up to fight off the water once more. In its retreat, the ocean stole some sand. There would be another attack soon, always different from the last. Ellen could watch for hours, but now she turned, saw her mother standing back on dry ground, shading her eyes.

"Watch this, Mom."

"I'm watching."

Ellen stood on the smooth-washed sand, readied herself, then thrust herself into a flip, turning in the air and landing on her feet again.

Her mother said, "Mmm," in a polite, detached voice.

"You've seen me do cartwheels, but that was without using my hands."

"Yes, very good." Her mother sounded very enthusiastic, but she had turned away and was walking back to the house.

Ellen watched her leave, feeling tricked again. How could she keep being tricked? Eighteen years, and she could still be so easily tricked into believing that her mother was really watching, really paying attention to Ellen's dance, flip, cartwheel, dive, jump, joke, anything. Ellen called after her.

"Mom, you going to change for the beach?"

"No, I'm going to call Dora. She's coming here for a few days."

"Why Dora? How much cleaner could this place be? You mean to clean?"

"To everything. See, I'm going home for a while."

"Why don't I just come home with you?"

Her mother turned back, looking at her with mild surprise. "The man . . . he's in Chicago now, but he could still come here. You still have to be careful."

"What about Dad?"

Her mother turned toward the house again, walking on. "He'll stay in San Francisco a while, now that the man is for sure in Chicago. He said something about hiring detectives."

Ellen walked about, kicking dry sand ahead of her. Once when she was six she had called her parents away from their dinner with, "Watch this dance. It's for you." She had heard them mumbling compliments as she danced, but she concentrated on the music. It must have been too long a dance, because when she finished and looked up, they had gone back to their dinner. Once when she was ten she had decided to give her grandmother a dance for her seventieth birthday, to dance it there for her in front of an audience of aunts and uncles and distant cousins. When she finished, everyone applauded, and her grandmother kissed her. But then her mother handed a gift to her grandmother, saying, "This is from Ellen too." It was a shawl. Her mother hadn't told Ellen that she was getting her grandmother another present, that she thought the dance wasn't really enough of a gift. How many times at a matinee movie had she turned from the screen with tears or with laughter, wanting to share the moment with her mother, but her mother wasn't really watching, or else she wasn't even there, and it was Dora, and Dora was sleeping.

Dora. At least with Dora here she could call her friends in L.A. Dora wouldn't tell her parents. Dora would just go to sleep. Dora could sleep through anything. Maybe she would do a dance for Dora. She kicked sand high into the wind. Or maybe she would do a dance for someone who would really appreciate it, someone who would pay attention and really stare at her and watch every move and never take his eyes off her. Maybe she would do a dance for Stephen Nye.

"He's been seen in Chicago," Ben Groff whispered to his wife. "Definitely spotted." Ben was putting away the groceries he had bought at the food and supply shop in Cranberry Lake. Every two days he borrowed one of the outboards and went to town to phone the Manhattan police department. There was a Sergeant Allison there who kept him up to date on the case. He would get his report, then come back across the lake to the small resort where he had rented a cabin. "They even spoke to him."

"To Nye?"

He nodded. He and his wife, Alberta, were whispering because their son, Donald, was in the cabin's main room, just a few steps away. Donald was twelve. They had not told him about Nye. They told him that this vacation was a surprise bonus his father had gotten because he had worked so hard on Operation Relocation.

"A Chicago cop spoke to him on the phone. He's insane. Chicago feels close to grabbing him, that's what Allison said."

"What're you guys whispering about?" Donald had called to them from the other room.

Alberta took Ben's head in her hands, stared at him. Some of the fear was gone from his eyes and he could actually meet her stare for a few seconds. He was trembling less but not really still, never still. "Hey," she whispered. "Chicago *will* get him. And we'll go home."

Ben nodded. They kissed. Then he took his pipe and his new tobacco and went to be with his son. He sat next to the boy, near the fireplace where Donald was arranging wood for a fire.

"What's going on?" Donald was stuffing pieces of newspaper into the sticks and logs.

"I called the hospital from town. Op-Re is going on without a hitch."

"So why whisper? Hey, look at this wood."

"I see it."

"S'perfect. Going to make a perfect fire." Don walked on his knees, closer to the fireplace. "Downdrafts and updrafts and plenty of kindling or kindlin' as they say, and newwwspapah in just the right places. Here and here and there and there, *and* . . . pine needles for da smell. It's gonna smell like Christmastime. Ding dong. Jingle. *Also!*" He cupped his hands to his mouth and sounded like a P.A. system. "One broken-up footstool that Mommy cracked, and that we're burning so we don't have to payyy for iiiit."

Ben laughed and suddenly hugged the boy, hugged him hard and scared him a little.

"Hey! Help!" Don made a joke of it. "He's got me! The mad bone-crusher! I'm . . . Arr! Argh! Crackensnapandbreak!"

Ben's voice was thick, and his smile was too close to tears. "I need a wonder hug."

"Wonder hugs are oldy old stuff, Dad. The kid's gone big time now. The kid's a preee-teeen, as they say." Don tried hard not to show it, but he was scared for his father. He thought his parents had lied to him about the vacation being a bonus. He thought his dad had been fired because he was so nervous. He thought his dad went to the store to call about new jobs. He thought his parents whispered about all those new jobs he wasn't getting.

"Just give me a matcho, and watch this. The kid knows what he's doing at all times. Match."

Ben handed a book of matches to the boy. "You want to go fishing early tomorrow?"

"Will you be up?" His father never fell asleep until almost dawn, and his mother was often up with him, so his parents slept until ten. Don was up by seven-thirty or eight, trapped in the cabin, angry and wondering why his parents wouldn't let him fish alone from the bank of the lake.

"You go, whether we're up or not."

"Hey, aw-right. The kid goes fishing alone. Don't worry, if I see a bear, I know what to do. Scratch his back. They love it." He struck a match and lit the fire. "Perfecto!" Alberta applauded from the kitchen. Ben put a trembling hand over his mouth and fought against crying.

———

Every morning, Dela arrived at the Kings' apartment with officer Carla Rodriguez. Dela drove Dan King to work. Officer Rodriguez stayed all day with Claire. There was always one policeman in the lobby of the apartment building, day and night. There was always one policeman in Dan King's outer office during working hours. At five-thirty, Dela picked up Dan King at work and drove him home. He relieved Rodriguez and stayed with the Kings until the nighttime guard arrived.

This had been going on for one week. Claire was

learning Mexican cooking from Carla. They cooked and they ate. Both were gaining weight. Dan called his wife when he arrived at work, when he finished lunch (which he had in his office with the cop), and just before he left for home. There was now very little to talk about during their hours alone before sleep. Each one knew all about the other's day. Each one knew exactly what was on the other's mind.

"We've got enough saved to live for six months in upper Michigan."

"Anyone who would go voluntarily to upper Michigan for six months deserves to be murdered."

"Please. Please! Don't joke, Dan. There are fifty places we could go. You could get another job. We could change our names. It doesn't matter. We could just leave. Come back when they catch him."

Dan sighed. They had had this talk before. Different words on the same theme. "We could go. He'd just go on to the next family. He'd go after Ben Groff and his family."

"Their problem."

"Yes. Then Frank Skate in California."

"His problem."

"Yes. But . . . they both have kids. I don't have a kid." He turned to his wife. They were in bed, the pillows propped up, light still on. "All through my marriage with Jean, about once a year, we'd talk about having a kid. We'd decide not yet. Things were too stormy between us. Things were always stormy. If we had said yes, I'd have a son or daughter, and I'd be running off to Tibet with my child, or even upper Michigan. But I'm the one with no kids. If anybody is going to go through this, try and make that guy . . .

come out in the open and get caught . . . it *should* be me, Claire. It should be." There was silence a while. Then Dan said, "You could go away a while."

"Oh great. Go away and worry. Of course I won't go away."

The subject was closed for twenty-four hours. She turned out the light. He moved over and held her.

"Ahhhh shit." Dela had sworn as part of an early morning yawn. He was sitting next to Dan King in the back of an unmarked police car. Bridger was in front, driving.

"What're you thinking," Dan said.

"Wish we'd gotten his money. Hope he gets mugged. He's carrying fourteen grand or so."

"Be one surprised mugger," Bridger said, and he laughed.

"What good would it do?" Dela turned away from him, looked out the window. He didn't seem to like being questioned by Dan. Didn't talk much. "What good would it do if he got mugged?"

Dela kept glancing out the windows, kept his hands in his coat pockets. Dan wished he'd keep his hand on his gun, wherever his gun was, and he wished he'd answer him. Dela always seemed to be thinking about something more important. "Damn it, Dela, talk to me! I'm cooperating with you guys. It's my goddamn life on the line every day. The least you could do is talk to me!"

Bridger smiled into his rearview mirror. Dela glanced at the mirror, then he looked at Dan. "If he lost his money, he'd have to find a job, scrape for a living. It would be harder for him to hang on. He'd be under pressure. He'd have to meet more people. Somebody might catch on, inform on him. The word is out on him. Okay? Understand?"

"I want to know everything," Dan said. "I want you to explain everything. I need to hear it. It helps."

Dela yawned again, his eyes staying alert, bouncing from one side of the street to the other. "Okay . . . let's see. Your parking garage at work. That's the most likely place for him to try for you. Maybe your parking place at home. Either one. Oh yeah, next week, you'll start driving yourself to work. We'll tail. Not us, but somebody undercover. It'll look like we're loosening up, giving up on him. We won't be. We'll be right on top of you. But the play might bring him out. Okay? What else? Bridge?"

"That's all we got to say."

"Okay." Dan sat back. "I just want to be kept informed."

Bridger smiled again, and Dela turned to Dan with a painful expression that passed for his own rare grin. He stared at him a moment and said, "You're doing fine, Dan."

Bridger nodded as he drove. "The man is o-kay."

Claire made the burritos. "They're no good," she said.

Carla Rodriguez tasted another bite. "They're great."

"They're no good."

"They're as good as mine. Better!"

"They're too mild."

"Claire, you *like* them mild."

"They should be hotter."

"They're fine!"

There was a knock on the door. The women were silent. Carla pointed toward the bedroom. Claire nodded, went in there. Carla walked toward the door. She stood beside it, her back to the wall. She pulled out her snub-nosed revolver and spoke through the door.

"Yes?"

"It's the Laskys."

Carla thought she recognized Mr. Lasky's voice, but she wanted to be sure.

"Who?"

"It's John and Natalie."

"Just a minute." Now Carla looked through the peephole, saw the Laskys, who looked relaxed, saw no one else. She glanced toward the bedroom and nodded to Claire. Then she let the Laskys in, keeping her revolver out of sight.

The Laskys wondered if Claire wanted to go food shopping with them. They often shopped at the market together. The Laskys were the couple that Stephen Nye had seen and had followed to the food store. Claire looked over their shoulders at Carla, who shook her head. Claire said no thanks, and the Laskys left.

Ten minutes later Claire was on her way downstairs to get her clothes out of the dryer. Carla walked her to the elevator and went down to the lobby with her where they met officer Bendahl. Bendahl went into the laundry room with Claire. Carla went back upstairs.

Bendahl left the door open so he could see the

lobby. Claire folded her clothes. They made small talk. She called him by his first name. He called her Mrs. King. "Just a minute, Mrs. King." Someone was being buzzed into the lobby. Bendahl stepped to the doorway to see who it was. The first thing he looked for was height. Nye was six-feet-two, and that couldn't be easily disguised. He might come in with a long beard, might come in as a woman, but he would come in tall. It was a man, a tall man. Bendahl relaxed when he recognized Mr. Lasky. He knew most of the tenants on sight. "Wait a minute, Mr. Lasky. Got a passenger for you." Bendahl walked Claire out of the laundry room. "Why don't you go up with him, Mrs. King." Lasky pushed the UP button, and the elevator door opened. Bendahl went back to his chair.

"Forget something, John?" Lasky let her step into the elevator, then he came in and turned to the controls. The door closed. "Is Natalie doing the shopping today?"

Stephen Nye could barely move. He forced his hand to rise, forced his finger to push 6, the building's top floor.

"John, you okay?" When she said that, Claire really looked at John Lasky's back and realized it wasn't John Lasky. Her body jumped with a kind of electric shock, and she moved back, banging her heels against the elevator wall. Her mouth opened and she made a noise like singing, low singing.

Stephen Nye had practiced for a week how he would fix his hair and fashion the mustache, and how he would dress and how he would walk, how he would enter the building and knock on her door, how she would look through the peephole and let him in because he was the tall stooped man she shopped with, the man with the brown coat that was too long and the black mustache that needed trimming, the tall sagging man who was her neighbor and her friend. Now, instead, she was there, behind him, her low moan building to a scream. The scream tore him loose from his fear, made him move. He whirled on her and she threw the basket of clothes. He lunged through flying pieces of cloth, reached and grabbed her sweater as she pulled away. He held on to the material with one hand as she lurched from wall to wall, screaming and stumbling over the clothes on the floor, crashing against the sides of the small, steel cube.

Her voice screamed without words, but her mind said, This won't happen, this won't happen, this won't happen. He won't get me. He won't. He won't. He won't. Help me help me help me help me!

Nye's free hand was drawn back for a blow. He pulled her and she stumbled, and for a second her face was before him, and he struck with all his might, breaking her nose, ending her scream. She bounced off the wall and fell on all fours, stunned. He lunged at the controls, hit the STOP button, waited, panting and trembling. The elevator stopped. The door didn't open. He looked at her. She began to moan. Blood dripped from her face onto the scattered clothes. He stood over her a few seconds, hesitating. Then she suddenly raised her head and looked at him and opened her mouth to scream. He grabbed for her throat, going down on his knees, holding her neck, her chin, trying to get his thumbs to her throat as she twisted and kicked.

She was full on the floor now, and he straddled her, looming high above her, sitting on her chest, trying to stop her from twisting away. She almost got her teeth into his hand, but the hand slipped down to her throat. She screamed inside. He won't he won't he won't he won't he won't he won't!

He pressed his thumbs deep into her windpipe, his teeth bared. The singing came from Nye now, a high-pitched chanting that matched his rocking motion as his hands held her throat, lifting her head off the floor and banging it down again, and again, as his knees squeezed her body between them, as his thumbs cut off the last of her air. He felt her struggling change to uncontrolled spasms and then stop. He closed his eyes and rose up on his knees so that his arms could be stiff out in front of him, his elbows locked, his hands quivering with the power.

His chest filled with a long breath. His head slowly tilted back. His eyes remained closed. He smiled.

"Out again, Mr. Lasky?" Lasky nodded and seemed to hurry past Bendahl and out of the building. A few moments later Mr. and Mrs. Lasky entered the building with groceries. Bendahl greeted them and was about to kid Mr. Lasky about going in and coming out so many times when he realized Lasky looked different somehow. It gave him a strange feeling. He walked to the elevator with the Laskys and pushed the UP button. The door opened to reveal a dead body covered by shirts and dresses and towels and underwear.

Dan King was writing a sales letter. He liked doing it, and was very good at it. He was feeling pleased about his opening sentence when his door opened, and he looked up to see Dela standing in the doorway, wearing an expression that could mean only one thing. One thing. One.

The men stared at each other. Dela stepped in and began to speak, and Dan suddenly put his hands to his ears and stood up. He shook his head, turned away from Dela so quickly that he upset his desk chair. He stumbled over it and moved across the room, holding his ears. He couldn't stop moving. He couldn't let his hands down. He couldn't let that information in, that news that Dela had brought. As long as he kept moving and holding his ears, it wouldn't be true, it wouldn't have happened. He knocked over a plant, bumped a table. An ashtray shattered. His secretary came to the doorway and watched, stiff and wide-eyed, a police officer stood beside her. Dan tripped and stumbled and kept moving. Dela walked to the door and slowly closed it. Now they were alone. He stared at Dan and didn't speak, didn't try to stop him. Dan finally stood still in front of Dela and brought his hands down. He stared at Dela's eyes, at the pain and sorrow and shame there. He read his news there. He let it in. It had happened. It was true. His face twisted into crying, great sobs that weakened him, staggered him. Dela walked him to the couch and sat next to him. They sat there for ten minutes. Bridger came in. He looked at Dan, then at his partner. Dela was staring off.

"Del, we gotta go. They'll take him home."

Dela didn't look at Bridger, he just slowly shook his head. Bridger stared at them a while, then he left, closing the door very softly.

11

"WHAT IS IT?"

"Pouilly Fuissé."

"You say that so sweet."

"Fuck you."

Bridger tasted the wine. "Mmm, smooth."

Dela lay on his couch, his eyes closed. "What? *What is it?*"

"Smooth."

"Smooth? What the . . . What in . . . What the fuck

do you know? Smooth! You couldn't tell . . . You dumb jungle-bunny asshole, you drink so much cheap apple wine your mouth is blind, you fuckin' nigger."

Bridger laughed until he cried. His big shoes rose up and slammed down on the floor. He rocked back in a chrome-legged chair that was too small for him and almost tipped it over, laughing in a high giggle, stopping, starting again. "Mouth is blind!" Giggling.

The Pouilly Fuissé was their third bottle of wine. Dela was drunker, or at least trying harder. Neither was drunk enough to stay off the subject for very long.

"You talk to your sister about it," Bridger said.

Dela still had his eyes closed. "Lucy?"

"You talk to her about leaving?"

"I told her."

"You *told* her. That's the trouble with you, dumb honky asshole jackass . . ."

"You've never *seen* a jackass in real life, fucking ghetto bastard . . ."

"You *tell* people. You tell everybody. Why don't you *ask* people? Ask your sister what she thinks about it. She's family, man. You go to family first and you *ask*."

"I don't ask her about my *job*, you . . . completely dumb person."

"This isn't your job, dude. This isn't police business. This is you throwing everything aside to chase some psycho across the country."

"*Leave*," Dela said. "*Leave*, nigger, I'm just on *leave*."

"Nigger? You're a white nigger, motherfucker. This ain't 'leave.' You're going hunting. It's personal, and the department hates that."

"I'm fucking consultant on this case to the fucking Manhattan police department. That's what the paper says."

"Then it *lies*, sucker. It's a fucking hunt and everybody knows it and it'll turn your career to shit. You think you'll make lieutenant if you go off now, go to New York? Even if you shoot the prick. You think you'll make lieutenant?"

"It's settled."

"Bull-*shit*, man." Bridger moved angrily, shifted his big frame in that little chair. "You can change it. What the hell is so fucking important?"

"Getting him. Getting his ass." Now Dela opened his eyes. "Catching him, dummy." He sat up. "Stopping him before he gets the next one. Grabbing him, Bridge! Grabbing the fucking maniac by the throat and saying, 'Hey! Gotcha!'" He grabbed into the air and made tight fists. "Gotcha! *Gotcha, motherfucker!*"

"Easy, man . . ."

"The crazy bastard. He got around me, Bridge. He got past me. He out-thought me."

"He got lucky, too. He . . ."

"He got her 'cause I was wrong! I thought he'd go after the man! I said, 'Stay in town. Draw him out for us and we'll get 'im, and you'll have your peace of mind.' I said that, Bridge!"

"You set it up good, Del. You covered it . . ."

"Shit! It was shit! It didn't work! I should have done it better. I should've been more scared of that bastard. I should've kept the woman covered every minute. But I didn't, and he got her. He got his hands on her and squeezed the life out of her, Bridge!"

"A fucking psycho! Damn it, Del, we've been there

before. That guy who got three nurses before we got him. That somebody, hey, that somebody who went along the lake with a fucking ice pick. Four people and we *never* got his ass and you didn't take any goddamn stupid-ass *leave*, dummy!"

Dela thrust himself off the couch, went to his knees, his hands pressing on the coffee table, face lunging at Bridger. "He talked to me! I've got his voice on the phone, talking in my head, Bridge! I've got . . . I've got Dan King looking at me, staring at me. I got his face in my mind. It's fucking stuck there!"

Dela stayed that way, face pushed at Bridger, muscles drawn tight, eyes wide. Then he drew back, embarrassed he had gone so far. He sat back on the couch, looking down, rubbing his sweaty palms on his knees.

Bridger stared at him a long time. He had never seen this deeply into Dela. He had seen his almost constant anger, his toughness, his humor too, but never this. Dela had been marked by Nye. Dela had been challenged and beaten, and he was raging to fight again, desperate to win. Bridger stared, then he slowly stood up and turned to leave. He spoke on his way out. "You get the fucker, Del."

The sun was going down slowly in Laguna Beach, California, leaving a stain on the Pacific and a mark where it had burned the sky. Ellen was watching from the roof of the beach house. She had found a way to crawl up there from the window of her room. She heard her name suddenly booming through the house and almost fell off her perch.

"Ellen!" Her father was supposed to be in San Francisco. She heard him knock below and hurry into the room, and she imagined the scene, the empty room, open window. She laughed.

"Ellen? Where is she, Dora?"

She climbed in through the window, but her dad had already left, gone to bang on bathroom doors.

"El?"

"Here, Dad."

"Where?"

She walked into the hall as he turned and came toward her, not actually looking at her. "Where were you?"

"On the roof."

He wasn't listening. He walked by her, shouting, "Dora, I found her."

She followed him toward the living room. "What's going on?"

Dora was just hurrying in from the patio. She was short and thick, a solid rectangle of a woman, dressed in a white uniform. "I can't find her, Mr. Skate."

"I found her."

"I found myself," Ellen said. There was a large, overweight man standing at the window, looking out. Her father was walking toward him.

"Mr. Cross, this is Ellen."

Cross turned and smiled like Santa Claus. He was fifty or so, almost bald. Her father was moving to the front door as he spoke to her. "He'll stay here a while."

"Dad! What's going on."

Her father turned at the door. At last his eyes settled on her. "He killed the one in Chicago. He killed Dan King's wife. They think he's on his way to New York now but . . ."

Her father let the sentence dissolve into silence. He was halfway out the door. Cross had moved to another window. Dora covered her mouth with a hand, eyes wide. Ellen stared at her father and saw how shaken he was, saw why he was hurrying away, why he couldn't really look at her for very long. He was guilty. Because of something he had done, a murderer was after his daughter. Frank Skate never admitted being wrong. He fought against blame and guilt. He lied. And when he couldn't lie, he just ran away. He was running now.

"I'm going to your mother's. I'll see you tonight. Mr. Cross is a detective." He closed the door. Cross turned slowly and looked at Ellen. Dora sat down.

"Private detective," Cross said.

Ellen turned to him, wondering why he was so peaceful and why was he twinkling at her like that, his eyes smiling. Didn't he know she was going to die?

Ben Groff was crossing Cranberry Lake as fast as his outboard would go. Even faster. His will was knifing through the water, cutting a wedge ahead of the boat, pulling the boat behind it. He willed himself home.

Nye was smart. Nye knew what he was doing. He hadn't killed Dan. He had killed his new wife. He had left him to suffer. He wanted all five of them to suffer. He would come after Donald.

The policeman on the phone had said they were almost certain Nye would come to New York next.

"But I don't see how he could possibly trace you to that cabin. We'll get him here, in the city."

Groff didn't believe him. At his feet, across the bottom of the boat, lay a new shotgun and a box of shells. Groff believed Nye would come there. Somehow he would come—because twenty years ago Groff had struck a match and started a fire, because Groff had never saved anyone's life and never written that letter. He would come.

"But I won't let you hurt my boy!" Groff shouted into the sound of the outboard. "I won't! Hear me! Hear me!"

He willed himself home.

Elaine Glorfeld made some coffee and sliced a small cake and waited for James Dela. He had called that morning from Chicago.

She finished slicing and placed the knife on the cake dish. The sound of the silver touching the china plate was an explosion in that quiet house, a great sharp sound that crashed into her brain and settled behind her right eye, intensifying the pain there. She had had the headache for hours. She was sure it was from the tension of waiting. Dela was only a policeman bringing more questions, bringing a notebook or an empty tape to catch her answers. Why did she feel as if Stephen were coming? Not the old Stephen. The new one. The monster Stephen. The murderer Stephen. She would open the door for James Dela, and in would rush the giggling killer Stephen. He would dance around them as they talked. He would be loose in her house. He might break things.

She walked into the living room and snapped on the lamps. Light struck the backs of white ceramic elephants and ivory chessmen, shone in the high polish of the tables and shelves, made shadows of the leafy plants that stood so green and so upright, all the death cut away, all the soil carefully fed and watered. These were her things. They gave her comfort, and she gave them care. She protected them from dust, and she would protect them from ghosts and monsters. If the presence of the killer Stephen entered her house, he had better take a seat. He had better not disturb a thing. He had better simply wait until the visit was over, and then leave with the policeman Dela. She would keep no monsters in this house.

Dela liked the gables and the roof that made him think of the word *cottage*. What the fuck was a cottage, anyway? Whatever it was, Elaine Glorfeld's house looked like one. The walkway was a series of round flagstones in the grass, like stepping stones across a stream. He rang the doorbell, glancing about at flowers on trellises. He wanted to remember to look up the word *cottage*. Elaine opened the door.

"I'm Jim Dela."

"Come in."

He had no tape recorder, and he kept his notebook in his pocket for now. She led him into the living room, and he sat while she went for the coffee and cake. He had time to study the room. This was what he wanted for himself. He knew that just by looking. He also knew he could never have it. It didn't have to do with money. You can't buy a place like this, he thought. You have to grow up in it. He wished he had been the child to find its secret places, to play on its floors and window sills, to make worlds of its closets and corners. This was a house to stay in, to play in all Saturday long.

"Do you have any kids?"

She sat across from him and poured his coffee as she spoke. "I married a man with teen-age children, two girls."

"They grew up here?"

"Hm? Yes, the girls grew up here." As she said that, her eyes flicked to the wall. Dela saw a cluster of photos there, some very old. He stared at the girls who had lived and played in this Saturday cottage. He was glad someone had.

"Is that a photo of Randal?"

"No, that's my son-in-law." She paused. "I have no photos of Randy. I found I couldn't look at his picture without thinking of the accident—even his baby pictures. I left them all with Stephen."

She seemed to relax. She had spoken his name. She had begun it. "So, he's killed three now," she said.

"Yes."

"Two children and now a man's wife."

"Yes."

"Two more to go."

He nodded. "Donald Groff, twelve years old, and Ellen Skate, eighteen."

Her eyes left him a moment. "What can I tell you?"

"Tell me if you *want* me to catch him?"

"What do you mean?"

"He's getting back at the men who . . ."

"*Of course* I want you to catch him."

"Randal was your son, too . . ."

"This has nothing to do with Randal!"

Dela stared at her, then he sat back, pulled out his notebook and clicked his pen, waited, watched her until she went on.

"He's not avenging the death of our son. He's out there . . . getting back at people he always hated, people he was always afraid of."

Dela didn't write anything down. He still watched and waited. Elaine leaned back. In a moment she spoke at the ceiling.

"Quiet Stephen Nye, mild and wishy-washy Stephen. He had an anger inside. He was a bitter man with a kind of fury inside."

"For who?"

"Just about everybody."

"Why?"

"Because he was afraid. He was afraid of people, afraid to connect with them, to . . . compete with them, afraid of coming into conflict. He dreaded conflict. He never argued, not outside the home. He was afraid." She brought her head off the back of the couch, brought her eyes back to Dela. "So was I. We protected each other. It felt . . . comfortable. But I never had his anger. I learned about that. You're not having any coffee."

He shook his head.

"And you're not taking notes."

"Keep talking."

She sighed, looking about, gathering up memories, fragments of old sentences, pieces of scenes. "We'd come home from work . . . I taught, too, a different school. We'd come home and hold each other. We'd both be . . . wounded, battered around by people.

We'd hold each other. When you're two cowards alone together, you're not cowards anymore. You erase the outside. You try to. But . . . it's worse for a man. He's supposed to be brave or to act brave. Stephen couldn't, and he knew I didn't expect him to. I understood. But I didn't hate the way he did. God, how he hated them all, passively. Always a passive, buried hate. I saw it come out. I saw it naked when Randy was growing up, when the boy was starting to connect with people. Stephen did everything he could to close a tight little circle around that boy, that poor boy. He even tried to close me out. Randy was born so that Stephen could have a friend. He had never had a real one. Not even me. I didn't qualify. Randy. Randy was Stephen's second chance. He nearly smothered the boy." Her voice cracked. Her eyes were locked on her thoughts. "He tried to make Randy hate as hard as *he* hated. I fought that. For the first time in my life, I fought. Randy *didn't* hate. Randy loved." Two tears were gathered at the corners of her eyes. She blinked, but they remained. She sighed, and the tears fell. She didn't touch them. "When Randy was killed, there was no reason to stay together. We had been enemies for years, and then the war was over. We had both lost."

12

S TEPHEN NYE picked up the phone and felt the power humming in his hand. The phone was his connection. The telephone lines were a spider web, and both of his flies were in it. Tangled tightly in one corner was Ben Groff, clutching his son. On another sticky thread huddled Frank Skate, making himself small, holding on to his daughter. The police had warned both of them, and they had moved by now, had traveled suddenly to some new place, erasing their tracks. But they wouldn't want to lose contact. They would need to keep in touch. They would remain somewhere within the great global mesh of wires. Nye was the spider, heavy with poison. He felt their weight in his web. He smiled as he dialed.

"Crescent Park Hospital."

"I'd like to speak to Benjamin Groff."

"One moment please."

"Administration."

"I'd like to speak to Benjamin Groff."

"Mr. Groff isn't here. I'll see if his assistant is in."

"Community Relations. Good morning—or afternoon. Let's see . . . afternoon! I hope you're having a good one." Pegi Stanton had a smile in her voice. It made her words curl up into crisp happy sounds. "Can I help you?"

"I'd like to speak to Benjamin Groff."

"Oh, I'm sorry. Mr. Groff is on vacation. I'm Pegi Stanton, his assistant. Can I help you?"

"I really need to speak to Groff. Do you know when he'll be back?"

"Hmmm, I'm not really sure. It's a kind of leave-of-absence vacation. But I'm handling all community relations areas now."

"There's no way I could reach Groff?"

"He *does* check in once in a while. Could I have your name?"

Nye's smile was secret, mute. His voice was level. "You have no idea where he's vacationing?"

"No." The cordiality was gone, swallowed. Pegi was remembering what the police had told her. "May I have your name in case he checks in? Where can he reach you, Mister . . . ?"

"Never mind."

"Can I give him a message?"

"He'll get the message."

"Pardon?"

Nye hung up laughing.

Pegi's long thin finger rose in the air and came down on the phone button. She lifted the finger, heard the dial tone, and began pushing numbers. She called the police—Sergeant Allison. He wasn't in. She left a message that a man had tried to get in touch with Ben Groff. Allison had asked her to do so and had given her a photo of Stephen Nye, which was now in her desk drawer. She completed the call and went back to her workday, which she always organized into a numbered list. She had accomplished one through four. Five was lunch. She went to the cafeteria.

Pegi's name was Margaret. She had chosen the particular spelling of Pegi in high school, and she still dotted the *i* with a tiny smiling face. She liked smiling at people. She felt people needed smiles. She presented them to the people in the hospital hallway on her way to the cafeteria. She gave them hi-there smiles and hang-in-there smiles and I-don't-know-you - but - I - think - you - have - value - and - I - care - about - you smiles.

She was twenty-five, tall and very slender, and her smiles were pretty things. She smiled at her friends in the cafeteria and asked what sort of day they were having, and she was glad to listen to their complaints and their stories. She gave these people eye contact, full attention, and sincere interest. They knew her as a good friend. She made them feel good. She cared.

One of the newer interns asked her to dinner on Saturday night and she accepted. She hoped he would ask around and come to the date with an understanding of where she stood. She was a virgin. She loved Christ.

The next morning Pegi was hurrying through her apartment, snatching up her keys and purse and jacket, heading for the door, when someone knocked on it. She peered through the peephole, saw a man with his hand looming large toward the wide-angle lens of the hole. In his hand was a badge. He spoke through the door. "Miss Stanton?"

"Yes."

"Lieutenant Dela, police. It's about the call you received yesterday."

"Oh . . . yes."

Pegi opened the door and the man entered, pocketing his badge and glancing about. "Don't you have a chain on that door?"

"No, I . . ."

The man walked deeper into the room, looking about. "You should have a chain. You alone here?"

"Yes."

The man nodded, turning to her now. She hadn't noticed his eyes before. He seemed a bit old to be a detective.

"Please sit down, Miss Stanton."

"I was just on my way to work. Promise you're not going to make me late." She smiled, and the smile touched her words, curled them up at the corners. "If you do, then *you* explain to my boss. Okay?"

"Okay."

She sat, and he sat on the coffee table directly across from her, very close to her, their knees touching until she swished hers aside. He leaned his face even closer and spoke just above a whisper.

"I'm not a policeman."

Her smile faded as his grew. She stiffened and began to draw back, pressed herself against the bolsters of the couch. Stephen Nye put a finger to his lips.

"Shhh. Don't worry. I'm not a robber. I'm not a rapist. I'm only a murderer."

The corners of her mouth were curving down and her small chin trembled.

"But you're not on my list, Miss Stanton. I had a list of five, and it's down to two and you are not on it. You are only a tangent."

She closed her eyes.

"Look at me."

She opened her eyes.

"I want to see my words in your eyes. I want to be sure you understand. No harm will come to you if you help me. I don't want to come in here and end your life or even change it. When I leave you, I want to leave you whole. I'm just an episode, Pegi. I begin and end. I'm off on a tangent today." He grinned again. "Now listen carefully and answer my questions. All right?"

She thought she was nodding, but he only saw her stiffness and her trembling.

"All right?"

"Yes." She whispered. The use of her voice began a whimpering sound that came regularly with every quick breath, a squeaky sound, a puppy's voice.

Nye leaned close again. He spoke slowly and clearly, like a teacher giving a test. "Where is Ben Groff?"

Her large eyes went even wider. This was the man. She saw through his wig and mustache. This was the man in the photo in her desk. The puppy sound wouldn't stop. She tried to swallow it. She held her breath, then spoke. "He's on leave of ab . . ."

"I know. Where?"

The whimper again and again. "Nobody knows but the police."

"Why the police?"

"Because . . . somebody's after him."

He smiled a big, kind smile at his student. "Get it, Pegi? Understand now? I'm the one. *I'm* after Ben Groff. Understand?"

"Yes." The puppy sound ended. She breathed a long, shuddering breath.

"Now, what if you had to reach him? What would you do?"

"I would . . . call the police and they would have him call me."

"Do that, Pegi."

She stared at him a moment. He was nodding, smiling at her. "Yes. Please. Now."

She slowly began to move in small stiff jerks, placing her hands on the couch beside her, sliding over toward the phone table. He rose from the table and sat beside her, very close. She felt his weight, his bulk next to her on the couch, and it menaced her. She turned away from him, but she could feel him. He wasn't touching her, but she could feel the force of the man pushing at her, pushing through her thin clothes, pushing into her body and grasping her heart, holding it until it stopped. She reached for the phone and placed it in her lap. Her mind tumbled out a piece of a prayer. Holymarymotherofgod prayforussinners nowand atthehourofourdeathamen.

"Pegi . . . ? Convince the policeman that it's very important. Ben Groff *has* to call you. Soon. Something about work."

She nodded, picked up the phone. Then she put the receiver in her lap and covered her face with her hands. She began to cry.

"Pegi."

"I don't have the number." She was sobbing. "The number is at work."

"Do you know which policeman to call?"

Her slim back and small shoulders were shaking with sobs. "Yes."

"Then just look in the phonebook. Call the police and ask for him." His voice was soothing, mild. "Relax."

She stopped her tears, sniffling, opening the phonebook to page 1: FIRE POLICE RESCUE. She dialed. She asked for Allison, and they transferred her. Allison's voice was a great relief. She was doing her job. This thing was coming closer to being over. Let it be over soon deargodinheaven. Holy . . .

"It's very *very* important that I speak to Mr. Groff today."

"Today?"

"Yes. As soon as possible. It's . . . An emergency has come up at the hospital. I mean . . . in our office. I need to talk to him right away."

"Well . . . I'll try to arrange that he call you. Let's say noon."

"Sooner."

"Can't be. Will you be in the office at noon?"

"I'll . . . be home. Let me give you the number in case he doesn't have it."

Nye smiled. She was terrified but she was still thinking. She was smart. This could work. *She* could make it work.

Pegi gave Allison the number. He told her that unless he called her back she could expect a call from Groff at noon.

She hung up and stared at the phone in her lap. Noon. Three hours.

"Thank you, Pegi. Now call the hospital and tell them you're not feeling very well. Nothing serious. You'll probably come in this afternoon. All right? And look at me."

She turned, and forced herself to keep her eyes on Mr. Nye, her teacher.

"You *will* be at the hospital this afternoon. Understand? If you help me at noon, you'll be at your office at one o'clock, and your life will go on normally. I'll step out of your day and it will close behind me as if I was never inside of it at all. Do you realize what I'm saying? You're going to survive this."

She nodded.

"Good. Give me a smile."

She tried.

"Now call the hospital."

She called and said she thought it was just an upset stomach, and she'd be in after lunch. She hung up again, stared again at the phone in her lap. He rose and stepped away from the couch.

"Now stand up, Pegi."

She did, wavering a bit.

"Come here, please. I'm going to tie you up."

She stared at him.

"Don't be afraid. If you're tied up, we can both relax. I won't have to be watching you. Come on. I won't hurt you."

"I'll just . . . sit here and I won't move."

"No, Pegi, come here."

She did.

"Take off your stockings—your pantyhose. I need them to tie you with."

She closed her eyes and her hands came to her face. She slowly shook her head.

"Pegi . . ."

As she spoke she started to cry. "There's rope in the kitchen."

Nye smiled, laughed aloud. "Pegi, don't you believe me? Look at me, Pegi."

She made fists of her slender hands and placed them at her sides. She opened her eyes, blinking away tears.

He stared at her, a steady and confident stare. He had never looked at anyone with such sure strength before, not even at Randy or Elaine, and never a stranger, never even a student. He moved and her stare followed him. He absolutely owned the eyes of this young woman, and he took his time, and he smiled kindly. "I want Ben Groff, and that's all I want from you. Do what I say."

She was wearing a long wrap-around skirt. She reached under it and brought her hose down, being careful to leave her panties in place. She stepped out of her shoes and pulled off the hose. She didn't look at Nye. He came toward her and she held the loose ball of nylon toward him.

"Hold it for me," he said, and she looked up and shuddered and made the puppy sound again. He was holding a knife.

"I'm cutting them in half so I can tie your hands and feet. Hold them apart. Pegi . . ." She separated the legs and tried to keep from shaking.

He cut through the crotch and the waistband with a very sharp hunting knife he had bought the day before. He had bought it because it looked so frightening, much worse than a gun, he thought, with its big silvery blade and bone handle. Its purpose was to terrify Pegi Stanton. She whimpered, watching the blade, feeling the nylon separate with hardly a sound.

"Now lie down, please."

She did.

He tied her ankles with a clumsy knot. He helped her sit up and he tied her wrists. He took a bolster from the couch and put it on the floor for her to lean on. He took her shoulders and helped her lean back, feeling her body shaking under his fingers. He put the knife away.

"Comfortable?"

She didn't answer.

"Pegi?"

She kept her eyes closed and nodded. He pretended not to see it.

"Comfortable, Pegi?"

She spoke very softly, "Yes."

"What?"

"Yes." The sobs came again, shaking her there on the floor. He stood over her, watching her. She was crying quietly, keeping it inside, keeping her eyes closed. He studied her face, her smooth skin ashine with tears. He imagined her body beneath the sweater and long skirt. He traveled it with his eyes. He reveled in the realization that here before him was a young attractive woman who was tied hand and foot, and there were no consequences. He could do whatever he wanted to her, *whatever*. She was bound and he was free. In a few hours he would walk out of this place and disappear. She was tied, and he was free, and there were no consequences. His eyes moved up and down Pegi's slender body, and he smiled. Stephen Nye had no one to answer to. He was operating beyond the law, outside of the system. He could now break the windows he had always wanted to break and punch the people and smash the cars and scream the curses, and he could rape this woman, and he would, he decided. He would.

Ellen woke with a scream caught in her throat, choking her. She was face down, staring at her pillow, afraid to turn around. She had dreamed that Nye was reaching for her, and even now she felt him reaching. He was standing over her bed and reaching down slowly, his hand coming close to her hair. She would feel him any second now, his hand in her hair, wrenching her around to look at him. Look at him. Look. "Mr. Cross!" she screamed at her pillow. Her voice filled the room and she felt Nye retreating. "Mr. Cross!" He was still there in the darkness above her, his hand poised for her hair. The light clicked on and she turned over. Nye wasn't there. Cross was hurrying in, dressed in his underwear, holding a small revolver. He was panting, looking about. "Ellen, what?!" He went to her window.

"No. I didn't see anything. I'm sorry. I just felt him . . . I dreamed him. I'm sorry."

Cross nodded. "That's all right. I can understand that. Y' know we're all locked in. We're wired . . ."

"I know. I'm sorry."

"Don't be sorry." Cross stood in the doorway a moment. "You all right now?"

"Yes."

He clicked the light off, and Nye was there, and she understood. Nye dissolved in light, scattered into pieces too small to be seen. Darkness gathered him, made him solid again. "Mr. Cross?"

He came back to the doorway.

"Could you stay a while?"

He nodded, entered and dragged a chair to her bedside. He took the bedspread from the bottom of her bed and put it over him like a long shawl. "I'll stay till you fall asleep."

"Thanks."

But Cross fell asleep before she did, his round face going slack, drooping to his chest. Two rooms away slept Dora, unawakened by the shouting. Ellen looked at her clock. It was 6 A.M., and she was alone with Stephen Nye, waiting for the sun to burn through the window shade, dissipate the darkness, scatter that shadow man into a million pieces too small to be seen.

It was 10 A.M. in New York when Pegi opened her

eyes and caught Stephen Nye staring at her. She closed her eyes again and went back to her prayers. Please dear God make him not want me. He doesn't want me. He doesn't want to hurt me. Please, dear Jesus. She saw the face of Jesus in her mind and he was smiling at her, giving her courage. She felt Nye walking across the floor and she opened her eyes again. He was pacing, ambling about the room. He isn't going to hurt me, please, Jesus. Mary . . . Holy Mary, Mother of God. I'll talk on the phone, and he'll go away. He won't touch me. Hail Mary, full of grace . . .

Nye was planning just what he would do to her. He wanted to do it slowly, carefully, reading the fear on her face, watching it grow there—fear of him, fear of Stephen Nye. He would wait until after the call. He looked at her and she closed her eyes. He smiled. He was looking at her bare feet. He could tickle them. She was tied and he was free and there were no consequences. He could tickle her insane. He chuckled aloud at the freedom he felt and the joy and the awesome difference between his old life and his new, his old self and his new. As he paced about and quietly chuckled, he flexed his back, turned his neck unconsciously to ease the stiffness there. There was an almost constant pain. At first he thought it was bad mattresses or air conditioning. It wasn't. Stephen Nye, at sixty-three, was growing. His stature was changing. The curve of his shoulders and the droop of his neck were disappearing. He was already taller by an inch.

"Pegi, are you hungry?"

"No."

"Thirsty?"

"No."

"I'll untie you for a while if you need to use the bathroom."

"No."

"It's after ten. Do you have a family, Pegi?"

"Yes."

"Oh? Big one?"

"Two brothers and a sister." He was pacing, casual, looking about. She watched him, until he looked her way, then she closed her eyes. Her answers were soft and without much expression. She wished he'd stop. She wished she could go back to her prayers and to the smiling face of Jesus.

"Where do you come from?"

"Albany."

"Really? Your family still there?"

"Yes."

"I'm from a little city near Chicago. Do you write your family? Do they write?"

"Yes."

"Where do you keep their letters, Pegi? Hmm? Tell me."

She named the drawer in her bedroom, and he found it and spent nearly half an hour reading the letters and looking at photos. He came back into the living room with a photo and one envelope. "I have here . . . Bobby. Right? How old is Bobby?"

He showed her the photo of her brother.

"Sixteen." Her words were wary now, wondering.

"I have his name and photo and address. Now, Pegi, I want to show you something." He squatted near her, took something out of his inside pocket.

Clippings. Xerox copies of newspaper stories. He held them up for her to read. The copies were smeared and blotchy, but she read enough.

HAMMOND YOUTH KILLED
IN 20-YEAR VENDETTA

BEREAVED FATHER SOUGHT
IN 3 REVENGE SLAYINGS

Her eyes came off the clippings, rested on him, full of dread now. Bobby.

"With just names and addresses, Pegi, I've been tracking people down, finding them, and killing them. Even when they're warned. Even when the police are trying to protect them. They can't hide from me. I have two more on my list. You're going to help me get to one of them—Ben Groff. After you help me, I leave you alone." He waved the photo of Bobby. "This is my insurance. This is why I know you won't call the police. You won't try to warn Groff that I'm coming. You'll just go on with your life as if I hadn't passed through it at all. Because I'll be carrying Bobby in my pocket. Do you understand?"

She nodded.

"Do you?"

She whispered, "Yes."

"They killed my son, Pegi. Ben Groff built the fire and set the fire that killed him. What I'm doing is only the result of that action. I'm carrying out the prescribed *result* of that act that took place twenty years ago. You can't perform an act like that, like the murder of a boy like Randy, and not expect to pay for it. The whole universe is altered by that kind of act, and as the universe shifts and adjusts to make up for the absence of Randy, certain laws come down, certain *musts*. I'm only the echo. I'm the returning echo of Randy's screams. It's that natural—what I'm doing. It's that inescapable. It's all locked in place. The universe, Pegi; it's infinite. Somewhere in the universe these acts of mine are already accomplished— all five of them are finished. I'm just an echo, a natural force. And you can't escape an echo. No one can."

He stared at her for a full minute and barely blinked. She couldn't close her eyes or turn away.

"It's going on eleven, Peg. You rest now."

Pegi was praying for herself and for Bobby, for Ben Groff and his wife and son and for Stephen Nye. Love us and forgive us and help us and keep us safe. Dear God all of us. Please Jesus hear me and bless us all. The face of Christ smiled at her, a gentle understanding smile. Forgive me for all my sins. The face nodded. Forgive him and help him to change so that he doesn't hurt anyone please. The face nodded and came closer and whispered.

"Pegi."

She gasped as Nye lifted her to a sitting position.
"It's eleven-forty-five."

He cut through the nylon that held her hands. He moved the phone close to her on the floor. He brought her a pad and a pen and placed them near the phone. "Please listen, Pegi." He was taking off his tie, standing over her. "This is going to be the most important phone call of your life." He loosened his collar, brought a pillow to the floor and sat on it, close to her. He took the knife from his pocket again, took it out of its sheath. He also brought out the photo of Bobby. He held the knife and the photo in front of her face. "It's your job, Peg, to get me the name of the place where Ben Groff is hiding. You will get that information from him somehow and you will write it on this pad. Make up anything. Make him believe you need to reach him again, or to go see him. Tell him anything. Get the information. That will keep *you* safe. . . ." He moved the knife a little closer to her. "And Bobby safe." He moved the photo toward her face. Then he put the two objects down, out of her reach, but within his own.

She was rubbing her hands, her wrists, staring at the phone. "What if I can't?"

"What?"

"What if I try but I can't?"

He shook his head. "You will, Pegi. You'll get that information. You just will." He smiled; he squeezed her shoulder; he whispered. "You will."

The phone rang at eleven-fifty-one. Pegi had been staring at the knife lying unsheathed on her carpet, and the ring of the phone made her jump and cry out. The jangling bell and the steel knife edge were the same. They cut into her together. She covered her mouth, closed her eyes. The phone rang and she felt Nye touching her shoulder. He whispered.

"Now, Pegi."

She lifted the phone.

"Hello."

"Pegi?"

Nye gently turned the phone in her hand, moved it slightly off her ear so he could hear Groff's voice.

"Hi, Ben."

"What's the trouble?"

"I'm sorry."

Nye was kneeling behind her, very close to her. He whispered in her other ear. She felt his lips. "I want to hear him."

"What's up, Pegi?"

"Ben, I . . . can't hear you."

"I'm in a booth. Can you hear me now?"

Groff was speaking so that Nye heard those words clearly—"in a booth."

"Yes. I'm so sorry to trouble you like this." Nye's breath was on the back of her neck. His big hand held her shoulder. She felt the heat of that hand through her sweater. Her voice was shaky. "It's an emergency, or I wouldn't . . ."

"Tell me what the problem is?"

She hesitated. Nye's hand slowly tightened on her shoulder. His other hand touched her waist where the sweater had ridden up a bit, touched her skin. There were tears in her voice.

"I may lose my job, Ben. Something . . . There's a situation here." She faltered.

"What, Peg?"

"It's something . . ." She stopped again. Nye's hand left her shoulder, then came around in front of her, holding the knife. She closed her eyes. She felt his other hand sliding up under her sweater . . .

"Pegi?"

. . . his big hand, sliding up under her breasts, pressing her back against him. She felt something touch her stomach, prick it like a needle. She knew it was the knife point.

"There's something I . . . can't handle at work. Not

without you. If I could just see you for . . . just an hour. If I could please come where you are, Ben, please. I could come now or tomorrow or this weekend just for . . . I wouldn't bother you for long. I just need to see you!"

"Christ, Pegi! What's going on?"

"Something . . . Meyer thinks I can't handle, and I think he's going to fire me."

"What?"

"I need to see you." She squeezed her words to keep the tears back. "If I could just talk to you about it in person."

"You can't come up here, Peg; you just can't!"

Nye's hold on Pegi became a hug, his left arm wrapped around her, pulling her back against him. Ben Groff had said "up here." Pegi was doing her job. He whispered, "Good, Pegi. Yes."

"I need to, Ben. Please! Just for . . ."

"No, it's just . . . it's impossible for me to have *anybody* come here. You could be followed. Pegi, there's a crazy man after me and my family. I can't come back to town until they catch him, and nobody can come up here. Now tell me what the problem is. *I'll* call Meyer. I'll convince him you can handle it."

"No . . . no, you can't. Not now. First I have to have time to . . . work it out with you to . . . get your advice, Ben."

"Pegi, tell me as clearly and as simply as you can. Now. Tell me all about it."

The man's hand was hot and moist and spread beneath her breasts, tightening there, tensing and gripping that flesh as the knife point came back against her stomach. Still, she didn't speak. The tears were coming and she had no words with which to force them back.

"Pegi, please . . . what's wrong?"

"It's . . . there's going to be a strike at the hospital." She began to cry, and her stomach rose and fell quickly with her sobbing, rose to meet the knife and shrank back from it again and again. "Meyer said I . . . made mistakes, using the newsletter. Oh, I just . . ."

Groff was sympathetic. "Pegi . . . Christ. Try to calm down."

"I can't." The sobbing went on. "I'm sorry. I . . ." Then she choked the tears back, clutching at an idea. "Please, Ben, let me take a minute to stop crying. I can't talk. Please! Let me call you in two minutes, oh please." Nye gripped her even harder and the knife point broke the skin as he whispered, "Yes. Pegi, yes!"

"Please, Ben!"

"I'll call *you*, Peg, in two . . ."

"No, please! Give me the number and I'll call you when I can talk, oh please!" She was sobbing and screaming. "Please! Please!"

"All right. Jesus, Peg, Jesus, calm down. I'm so sorry you're going through . . ."

"I'll call you right back, Ben. I will. I will!"

"Yeah okay, the code is three-one-five and the . . . you ready?"

Nye released her and she sank. She fell to the carpet and reached for the pen, wrote the number as he dictated it. She finished and tried to speak, but she couldn't. She hung up and put her face down into her arms, sobbing into the carpet, big choking sobs.

Nye leaned over her, whispered.

"Thank you. Thank you, Pegi. I'm proud. *You* should be proud. You're smart. You're good, Pegi. Try to stop now. Try to stop crying because you *do* have to call him back. You have to call him back and explain why you're so upset. Do you want anything? Glass of water? Hm? Peg?"

His fingers pierced her hair and closed lightly on the back of her neck.

"Pegi, you have to call him back. All right? Ready?"

Her sobbing was finished. She was exhausted, too heavy to rise. She moaned, shook her head no.

"All right, then. I'll wait. Take another minute. We don't want him to leave the booth, though, right?"

Her legs were free. She hadn't felt the knife on the nylon. It was so sharp, so swift. The thought of the blade made her move. She pulled her legs under her and sat up. She covered her face a moment. Then she moved the phone close to her, dialed the number. Her voice was peaceful now, tired.

"Hello, Ben."

"Peg, whatever it is, I can help you work it out. Do you believe me?"

"Yes. Yes, Ben, I do. But . . . partly, it's just . . . I haven't been sleeping. So I . . . that's why I went to pieces, and I'm sorry. I really am. What I'm going to do . . . I'm going to put all my thoughts down, collect all my . . . thoughts and put them in a long letter to you . . ."

"I can't give you my address . . ."

"No, I'll give the letter to the police. I'll put it all down on paper."

Nye was smiling at her, loving her. Smart Pegi.

"Then I'll send you the letter, Ben, and tell you the

whole thing and . . . tell you just how you can help me. If you can."

"You know I'll help you."

"Yes. Thank you. I know. I'm sorry again, and I just . . . have to rest. I . . . I'm hanging up now."

"No. No. Wait, Peg. One thing. It's very important that you tear up the phone number I gave you. Okay?"

She looked at Nye for the first time during her conversation. He was smiling at her, sure and wise, victorious. She nodded as though Ben could see her. Then she spoke, her voice retreating, shrinking to a whisper.

"Yes. Ben, I will. Bye."

She hung up, looking at Nye. He began nodding. He kept nodding.

"I'm so proud of you, Pegi."

She drew up her knees and put her arms on them, rested her face on her arms.

"We've finished now," he said. He could see her long bare legs, and he thought again about having her. He felt the beginning of an erection. "All that's left . . . is to say goodbye. How should we say goodbye, Pegi?" He rose and went to her. He wanted to see her face when he told her his plan, when he explained to her how they would say goodbye. "I have an idea, Pegi." He touched her hair, then slowly wound his hand into it, took hold and gently pulled her head up and back. Her eyes were closed. "Open your eyes. I have something to tell you."

She opened her eyes, looked into his. He saw a great weariness there, and a resignation. He saw shame. He saw no fear.

"Pegi, I thought we'd say goodbye like lovers."
He saw no fear. Sorrow. And far, far down, some anger. But no fear. She had been swept up in a great white wave of fear, and the wave had carried her on its crest, tumbling her over and over, nearly drowning her, the wave had broken, and now she was calm. He stared at her a moment. His smile faded. His pleasure faded. He let go of her, and she lowered her head to her arms again. He picked up his knife, the pad with the number written on it. When he spoke, his voice was matter-of-fact.

"You'll go to work. You'll tell no one. If I get to where Groff has called from, and I find that he's been warned, that he's gone . . . I'll put Bobby on my list. I'll get Groff's child anyway, in time. There's no way to stop me. But if you warn him, I'll get Bobby too."

He left her apartment.

Her closed eyes saw the face of Mary, Mother of Christ. It was the face from a painting that had hung in her room when she was a child. She had had two holy pictures. The one of Christ pointing at his sacred heart hung in her bedroom now. The Madonna she had given away when she was nine years old. She had hung it in Bobby's room the day he was born. She had not seen the face of this Madonna for years, but it was sharp and firm in her memory. The face was troubled. Pegi said, "I'm sorry." Mary nodded. In a moment the face lighted to almost a smile, a sad smile. She understood. They prayed together—for Bobby, for Ben Groff and his family, for Stephen Nye.

In an hour Stephen Nye stepped into a phone booth and called the number on the pad. It rang a long time. When someone answered, Nye asked for a Walter Whitman. The man said he must have the wrong number because this was a phone booth.

"A phone booth where?"

"Outside the Lakeside Supply."

"Where?"

"Cranberry Lake."

Nye hung up and opened the phone-booth door, stepped into a bracing wind. He breathed deeply, walked quickly, feeling younger, feeling taller. The spider was on his way, high-stepping to a far corner of his web, heavy with poison.

13

HE HAD LIED to her, Pegi knew that now. Nye had said he would pass in and out of her life and not change anything. He had changed everything. He had left her alive, but not in peace. His knife had barely cut her, but it had driven deep into her mind, slicing through all thoughts, all memories, raising flights of fears like bats that had not yet settled.

He had not left her at all. He was there, resting on

the rim of her mind, watching and smiling, waiting, and she was waiting for him—at her door, in her car, on her phone, in her closet, under her bed. She had slept only a few hours in the last two days.

She called home from her office and made small talk just to hear the voice of Bobby. She asked him if he still had the picture of the Madonna. He said, "Yeah, I've got it, but it's not up. I've got it somewhere."

"Where?"

"In the closet, I guess."

"Will you put it up . . . just for a while? Okay?"

"Why?"

"For me, Bob. For a little while."

"S'everything okay? You sound like you're crying."

"I'm fine. Really. I just remembered that picture. I just happened to remember it."

"Well . . . all right. I'll put the picture up. I'll just stand it up on the shelf 'cause the wall's all full. Okay?"

"Sure. Thank you."

She had just hung up from that call when Sergeant Allison and another man entered her office. Her face went slack and her eyes were afraid.

Allison said, "Hi, Pegi, remember me?"

"Yes."

She was cold and stiff and Allison was disappointed. He had remembered her being so friendly, so funny. "Sergeant Allison. And this is Sergeant Dela from Chicago."

She couldn't help closing her eyes against the images that name brought. The images came anyway. Nye smiled and said he wasn't a policeman. He watched her while she hooked her thumbs into her hose and slid them down her legs. He thrust his hands toward her, held them close to her face, the knife in one and Bobby's photo in the other. He hovered behind her and pressed himself close and put his arms on her and touched his warm hands to her skin. All this rushed at her as her eyes fluttered open and she saw Dela staring at her. She tried to stop her words. She swallowed, bit her lips and found them trembling. Allison went on talking, but Dela only stared.

"Pegi, I'm briefing Sergeant Dela on the Groff case. He wants to know everything . . ." Allison noticed the two of them staring. "Everything about that phone call . . ."

Pegi had thought of something to say. She could ask them if they wanted coffee. She made the words in her mind. But Dela was staring at her as if he already knew. He was pulling the words from her, and she said, "He used your name . . . to get in. And he had a badge."

Allison said, "Who did?"

Dela said, "Nye."

And Pegi nodded slowly.

"Don't squirm, worm. I hate it when you try to . . . get away 'cause it reminds me what I'm doing is pushing a hook through your . . . Don't squirm— you'll be dead in a little while. Is a worm an animal? Dad?"

"Don't bother your father."

"That rhymes, Mom. Don't bother your father.

Don't squirm, worm. Hope I catch a perch . . . blerch. What rhymes with perch? *Search* me? Don't *lurch* off the bank, Frank, or you'll get wet . . . my pet."

"Donny . . ."

"Hope I catch a bass . . . my lass."

"Donny, won't all that talk scare the fish?"

"Fish are deaf, Mom. Did you ever see a fish with ears? My dears?"

Alberta Groff laughed quietly and shook her head. Donny could always make her laugh, even here, even now, with her husband stationed on a hump of ground twenty yards away, holding a shotgun and praying for his fear to take human form so he could shoot it.

The humor faded from her face. She sighed and leaned back against the tree that grew closest to the channel bank where Donny stood. "You know Dad wants it quiet when we're out." Donny was quiet then, and Alberta glanced behind them at her husband. He sat relaxed, his hands on his knees, the gun across his lap, but he moved his head at every sound. She turned to the dark water of the channel and thought of that puzzle that was only three weeks away now. What'll we do when the money runs out? If they haven't caught him? Borrow? Move? Where? Why? Stephen Nye was last reported in Chicago. Now he was probably in New York City, hundreds of miles away with no way to trace them. But Ben's fear was always just beyond his vision, around corners, behind trees and walls and shuttered windows, inside every shadow. The gun was always inches away from his hand.

She turned her head quickly at a splash, just a small splash made by Donny's bobber. Without turning, she knew that Ben had moved at the splash, had turned to look, had found the gun's safety with his thumb.

"All right, bass, move your ass. All right, fish . . . I want you in my dish."

"Donny, please."

Donald sat down on the bank, then lay down on his stomach, his chin on his hands. He watched his red and white plastic bobber floating on the still water. He tried to push everything out of his mind, leave nothing there but the water and the bobber and the possibility of a bite. The crazy man kept crowding in. Donny chased away the dark, faceless form, throwing rhymes at him. *Probably hundreds of miles away. Probably catch him today. And who could find us where we stay, so far away. Relax, Dad. It isn't so bad. Watch me catch our dinner. Your son's a winner.*

Tall can't be disguised, Ben Groff thought. He'll be tall, maybe even dressed as a woman, or looking young, or in goddamn blackface, but tall. He'll go for Donny. He won't see me. He'll go for the boy, and I'll lead him like a bird. I'll fire, and he'll go down. While Donny and Al are running away, I'll fire at him again to make sure. Then I'll go look at him, look into his face, spit into his dead eyes. I hate you, Nye. I'm sorry I never ever saved a life except maybe a thousand times in traffic. Being alert at intersections. Braking. Swerving to avoid . . . There may be hundreds of people alive right now because I never drink when I'm driving. Once I took a door off an abandoned refrigerator. I rip apart all plastic bags before I throw them away. Proof. You want proof. I have no proof.

But I'm sure, I'm *sure* people are alive today because of me. At least one, my God, one is a very safe estimate. Maybe I *will* write that letter. I'll explain. Proof. I have no proof, you bastard. But that doesn't mean you can hurt my child. I won't let you. Try it. Try it now. Right now. Please.

The bobber jumped in the water and Donny's chin came off his hands. He watched. The bobber was still. He relaxed. "Probably got my worm, you germ." He didn't really care. He would check it in a while. He watched a busy world of bugs, hopping on the water, floating there, dancing, tiny bugs the size of periods and commas. They disappeared when he changed his focus and saw the water now as a barely rippling reflection of pine and birch trees and blue sky.

The bobber sank, and Donny smiled and grabbed his pole. The bamboo was twitching, trembling in his fingers. He loved the feeling of life on the end of the line.

"Ben Groff!"

Donny dropped the pole, turned to his mother who had just jumped to her feet. They looked up at Ben and could hardly see him. He was down deep in the weeds, the gun to his shoulder.

It had been a man's voice, far away. Since the shout, the forest and the channel had become very still, hardly a bird, no wind. They heard Ben whisper.

"Both of you get down."

Alberta and Donald moved toward each other. She took his arm as they knelt and then lay on the moist ground. They looked at each other and barely breathed. Their surprised eyes said all this was real after all. The fear *is* a real thing. It has a voice.

"Ben Groff!"

The voice was closer, moving toward them along the channel. Alberta put an arm around Donny and gripped his shoulder and whispered, "Put your face down." She didn't want him to see that fear walking on long legs, talking, swinging arms that could hurt him.

Ben had flicked the safety off with his thumb and leaned his finger lightly on the trigger. He sighted along the barrel in the direction of the voice. His heart seemed to shake the ground under him and explode in his ears, weaken his arms and make the gun barrel waver. He held his breath.

"Ben Groff!"

The voice was coming slowly up the channel bank. There was a rise of land there, and over that rise would come their fear. Alberta hoped he didn't have a gun. She hoped her husband wouldn't miss. Ben hoped he would keep coming slowly and would be in the clear. Donny put his face on the ground and watched his mother, waited for her eyes to see the crazy man. Donny hoped he wouldn't find them, but then he knew he *would* find them because he heard a plop and a splash in the channel and he remembered. "The fish," he whispered. "The fish on my line."

Alberta and Ben both glanced at the pole lying on the bank, jerking with the movements of the hooked fish. The fish took the line as far as he could, then surfaced and splashed and dived again, panicked. They glanced from the pole to that rise of land. He would hear the splashing. He hears it now.

"Groff!"

Ben had once shot a pheasant, pulled the trigger on

a 12-gauge shotgun exactly like the one he held now, and changed the bird into an awkward broken bundle that fell straight down out of a gray sky. He held his breath and let it out slowly, blinked to clear his vision, and prayed for a shot as true.

The fish splashed, dived. The tip of the pole followed like a pointer.

"Ben Groff!"

Ben was on the hump of ground, and he saw it a second before Alberta—a hat, a wide hat coming over the rise of land, and now a face under it. Mustache. Shirt, a brown shirt. A uniform. The man seemed young and he wore the uniform of a policeman, but he was tall, and Ben placed the gunsight on the man's chest.

The man topped the rise, not shouting now, staring at the fishing pole that slid and rolled on the bank. He moved toward it.

Donny was reading his mother's face and he saw relief. He saw her tension crumble into crying. Then his father screamed.

"Don't move!"

The policeman turned quickly and stepped back off the bank, nearly lost his balance. One boot went into the water over the ankle. His hands went outward slowly, suspended waist high.

"Ben, my God, don't!" Alberta was standing up.

The policeman looked at her, opened his mouth. Then he glanced back at Ben, at the black circle pointing toward his own chest. "I'm a deputy! Sheriff's deputy!" His hands were far out from his sides. He looked to Alberta for help.

"Ben!"

Ben stood up on his knees, slowly, still aiming the gun. Donny rose also, staring at the deputy, at his frightened eyes. The fish was thrashing in shallow water, nearly exhausted, almost dead.

"Are you Groff?" He didn't wait for Ben's answer. "I'm supposed to get you moved. Sheriff sent me out to move you!"

The man was surely young, his face smooth above the mustache. Groff lowered the gun. "Why?"

The deputy brought his hands down and stepped out of the water. "Call came in from New York. The suspect is believed to be in the area—that's all I know."

Dela didn't care for water in which things lived. He never swam in lakes or oceans. He liked the feeling of cement under the water, liked the defined edges of pools, the smell of chlorine. He was knifing across Cranberry Lake, facing backward, looking at the wake of the boat, hunched up tight against the wind. He had to shout his questions to the deputy beside him.

"How far did you move him!?"

"How far?"

"Yeah!"

"From the south bank to the east bank of the lake! Isolated cabin there!"

"Could he have followed!?"

"Who?"

"Nye!"

"Nobody followed! He'd've needed a copter to follow us! No way he knows where we put them!"

Dela nodded. A deputy was staying in the cabin

that the Groffs had left. Others were searching the area watching for possible Stephen Nyes. The Albany police were keeping an eye on Bobby Stanton. Dela would stay with the Groffs and wait this out. He'd stay very close. He'd make sure this time. He'd stay between that family and Stephen Nye, and he wouldn't budge.

Dela made a wide circle around the cabin before he went in. He looked at it with the eyes of Stephen Nye. He found the approach that offered the most cover, and that's where he asked the deputy to stay through the night. He couldn't order him. He asked. The man agreed, bitching about how cold it would be without a fire. Dela said he'd be glad to trade places with him, except Dela didn't *know* the woods. The job needed someone who was at home in the forest. That seemed to please the deputy. He walked off like an old-time mountain man. The Indian fighter, Dela called him in his mind. Hawkeye.

The other cops were leaving, going back to the boat, when Dela approached the cabin. The deputies nodded as they passed, leaving the door open for him. Dela went in. Mrs. Groff and the boy were sitting on a bed in the main room. They looked afraid, expectant. Mrs. Groff smiled weakly.

"Hi." Dela closed the door and locked it, glanced at the windows. "I'm Jim Dela."

"They told us you were . . . that you'll stay."

He nodded, looking about, leaning into the kitchen. "Right. I'll be right here with you. Where's Mr. Groff?"

"In the bedroom," she said, and Groff called out. "In here." Before Dela went in, the woman whispered to him. "He doesn't sleep. He can't rest." Dela nodded, glancing past her worry to the face of the boy. Donald was small for twelve, neat and trim, a miniature man. His eyes were big and wondering. Dela turned and went into the bedroom.

Groff was sitting up in bed, dressed, his boots off. He held a pipe in his teeth, and he leaned forward now to shake Dela's hand. It was a firm shake, and Groff seemed in control, but when he took the pipe from his mouth, Dela noticed the man's hand was shaking. The stem of the pipe clicked slightly against his teeth a few times as he drew it out. Those little clicks belied the firm handshake and the smile and the attempt now to be the host.

"Hope you'll be comfortable here."

"Sure, I'll be fine."

"The couch in the other room opens into a bed."

"Thanks."

Alberta came into the room, spoke softly so Donald wouldn't hear. "Are they sure he's here?"

"No. But he could be. He traced you."

"How?"

"He forced Pegi Stanton to call you . . ."

Ben caught his breath, looking off, thinking. He put his pipe back into his mouth and held it there, tried to hold it steady.

"Do we move again now?" Alberta said.

Dela turned to her. "You decide. We're set up to protect you here. There'll be a man outside all night. I'll be here."

She nodded and looked at Ben. He was still staring off. She whispered to Dela. "Donny doesn't know. I mean he doesn't know that . . . he's the one Nye wants to . . ."

"Did he hurt Pegi?" Ben spoke without looking at them.

"No. She's all right."

Alberta said, "Thank God. What a sick man. What a . . ." She shook her head and went back to the other room, to Donald. Dela turned to Ben, but he was still staring unfocused, blinking, his hand trembling on the pipe.

"Do you chase guys in cars a lot?"

"No."

"Movies and TV, it's all car chases, crashing. You see *Freebie and the Bean*?"

"No."

"You watch cop shows?"

"Yeah. Some. I like . . . historical stuff."

"Swordfighting. Chu. Chink. Chu. Gyahhh."

"Don't wake your parents."

"You like the Japanese swordfighting pictures?"

"Yeah. The old-time ones. I like . . . You see *Dr. Zhivago*?"

"I don't think so. What's it about?"

"Russia."

"I think I saw it. You see *Royal Flush*?"

It was 6 A.M. Dela had slept a couple of hours and awakened to find the boy sitting up, watching him.

"What's this crazy guy all about? Twenty years ago his son dies, and he blames my dad? Weird. God. Boy, my dad is . . . He's really nervous. I think we should go home. We could have guards around us, booby traps on the door. Would you stay with us?"

"If your parents wanted me to."

"Weird guy. He's killed lots of people, right?"

"Enough."

"Nobody tells me anything specific, you know? I'd like a little specific information."

"Three. He's killed three people that we know of."

"God. Weird. Boy. He's a nut, right?"

"He's an asshole."

Donny laughed in a whisper, then giggled out of control and had to put his face in the pillow to muffle the sound. Dela smiled.

"I hope he gets shot in the ass," Donny said, plunging back into the pillow.

At 7 A.M. Dela's stomach was rumbling with hunger, but he didn't want to move around in the kitchen. He hoped the Groffs were asleep. He hoped that old Hawkeye was awake out there.

"You like school?"

"It's okay. Recently, I've gotten very serious about fishing. That's really what I want to do."

"Fish?"

"Be like one of those guys who takes people fishing. A guide. But I'd fish a lot for myself. Cook my food. You like fishing?"

"Nah."

"What d'you like to do?"

"I swim, work out . . . box."

"You're a boxer?"

"Just to keep in shape."

"Handy with your mitts."

Dela laughed suddenly, trying to smother the sound.

"Bite your pillow," Donny said, and Dela laughed harder.

At seven-thirty, Alberta came quietly into the room.

She had slept in her clothes. She had Ben's jacket on with the sleeves rolled up, and she was shivering. She whispered hello and kissed Donny good morning. They all went into the kitchen.

"He asleep?" Dela asked.

"No, but maybe he'll sleep now. He sleeps better in the day. Just quick naps."

They tried to make breakfast without making noise. Hawkeye knocked loudly at the door and startled them. He said he was chilled to the bone and he smelled coffee. The four of them ate in the kitchen.

"Wow, you were out there all night in the dark! See any bears?"

"No," Hawkeye said. He was in a bad mood.

"Wolves?"

"'Course not. Aren't any around here."

"Coyotes?"

Hawkeye put both hands around his coffee cup, ignored the boy. "Christ. I don't think I'll ever warm up. Damn *wasted* stakeout."

Dela didn't like Hawkeye. They ate in silence a while.

"Giraffes?" Dela said.

Hawkeye looked up, and Dela was staring at him, straight-faced. Donald laughed to tears, choking and coughing. Alberta pounded the boy on the back.

Hawkeye pouted. "How'd you like to spend a night out there?"

Dela stood up and took Hawkeye's still-full cup and plate from the table, walked into the other room.

"Where you going with that?"

"Shhh," Dela said. "Bring your silverware."

Hawkeye followed him. Dela put the plate and cup down on a table, then stared at the man, spoke quietly. "I don't want you near these people. You do your work through me. You talk to me. You complain to *me*. Not them. Understand . . . Hawkeye?"

The deputy grabbed his jacket and stalked out the door, slammed it behind him. Dela went back to breakfast.

At ten the shutters were open and the sun was warming the cabin. Donny was reading a schoolbook. Alberta and Dela sat at the kitchen table, speaking quietly.

"We don't know what to do. Ben has to work. I mean, we need money. I said we could go somewhere else for a while and I'll work. He's just too nervous to work. But he said he'd be too worried about me going out . . ."

There was a gunshot in the bedroom. Dela ran for the door, his hand slapping his open shirt aside and drawing his revolver. Alberta and Donny were standing, frozen.

The door was locked from the inside. Dela rammed a shoulder against it and it almost gave. He kicked at it, his teeth bared. The door swung open and he lunged into the room, squatting low, pointing his gun. Only Ben Groff was in there.

Dela was staring, slowly straightening up when he heard the rush of Alberta and Donald behind him. He turned on them and put his arms out, caught them at the doorway. "Wait! Wait! No." They pushed against him, bobbed their heads about to see. He walked ahead pushing them out. "No! Wait. Please. He's dead. Stay here!"

Alberta screamed a moaning, painful scream and grabbed Donny to her. Dela heard the deputy running toward the cabin door. He waited a moment. The deputy opened the door and stood there, his face questioning Dela.

"Groff shot himself. He's dead. Stay with them." Dela went back into the bedroom and closed the door behind him.

Groff was sitting up in bed, back against the wall, his head flopped over on a loose, lifeless neck. He had put the shotgun to his chest and pulled the trigger with his toe. His eyes were closed, and his face looked hardly at all like Ben Groff. To Dela, the face of a corpse was not the face of a person. Death wasn't sleep. It was something altogether different.

He touched nothing, looked about quickly, saw a note on the bed table. He stood over it, trying to read the very shaky scribble.

Alberta, I love you.

Donald, I love you.

Dear Mr. and Mrs. Nye,

> *Years ago I was responsible for the death of your boy. I've waited to write this until I could somehow replace that life. Today I saved the life of my son, Donald.*

Benjamin Groff

14

"LET ME SEE NOW, what's been going on? The garden . . . an off year, I'm afraid. Early frost. I'm growing brown plants and green weeds. But . . . just wait 'til June. A grand opening of roses. You're all invited. Bring the kids. Now . . . what else?" Elaine Glorfeld, the former Mrs. Stephen Nye, punched the STOP button on the tape recorder and thought of what else she might say to her stepdaughter. For years they had sent tapes instead of letters. What else now? She thought of Stephen, of course, thought of the murders, thought of Randy. These things she wouldn't speak of. She pushed down on RECORD. "I'm teaching a class in Illinois History. Adult Education. Starts next month. Don't say that. It is *not* boring. I have three—count 'em—three state legislators signed up for it." STOP. She heard the water boiling on the stove. She would sip an afternoon cup of coffee while she finished the rest of the tape. She rose, but the doorbell rang and made her hesitate. The stove or the door? She decided, and took quick steps into the kitchen, turned off the stove, poured the water into the cup as the bell rang a second time. She left the steaming cup on the counter and made those same quick steps to the door. She opened the door to an overburdened salesman. He carried a heavy satchel, an armful of papers. He was a handsome man, with eyes too old for his face.

"Yes?"

"Is? . . ." He stopped then, and just stared at her, a full, deep, and steady stare. His voice cracked a bit when he said, "Hello."

She very slowly recognized Stephen Nye. The hair was wrong, the mustache, and something else. He seemed taller. He smiled down at her.

"You know me, don't you?"

She nodded slowly, whispered, "Yes."

They stared a while. He studied her. He superimposed her face over the face of the Elaine he carried in his mind. He noted the changes, the lines. His smile was kind and his words gentle. "My . . . we're old, aren't we."

She only stared, wondering why she wasn't really surprised.

He chuckled. "I don't feel old, though. I have . . . a lot to tell you."

"I know," she said. "I already know."

His smile nearly vanished, not quite. He shook his head. "No . . . you don't. May I come in? You're alone, aren't you?"

She said yes, stepping back, allowing him inside. She closed the door, watching him walk into the living room, waiting for him to shrug off his disguise, return to the old Stephen, but he didn't. His walk had changed, his whole bearing.

He sat down and took his hat off, jovial now. "It's a wig, the sideburns too. The mustache is a phony. I'm getting very good at this. I have encyclopedias in here." He tapped his satchel with his shoe. "I've been up and down the block, going door to door in case they're watching your house. They won't suspect me. Their thinking goes only so far, I've found." He studied her a moment more. "You look very well. I said old before, but you've aged softly, Elaine. You look very well."

"And you're . . . very different, Stephen. It isn't the wig . . ."

"I know. That's what I have to tell you—all the changes. *Are* they watching the house?"

"I don't think so."

"Good."

She walked deeper into the room, keeping her eyes on him. "They said you were in New York."

"Finished there." He said that as he unbuttoned his suit coat and sat back, throwing an arm up on the back of the couch—like a businessman back from a meeting. Finished there. She thought about what that meant, and he saw her look darken. He shook his head. "No. Didn't touch a soul. Ben Groff, you remember, the boy who started the fire? He shot himself. I didn't touch a soul. One more to go. Only one. Remember Frank Skate? The handcuffs were his idea. His daughter is the last. San Francisco, as far as I know. I'll find them." He stopped and studied her again, enjoying this, being with her again. It brought back a flood of images, but they ended twenty years ago. Twenty years of her life was all but unknown to him. "I didn't hear until, ohh . . . months later that your husband had died. I didn't want to bring it all back with a call or a card." He paused, then smiled. "Two daughters."

"Yes."

"How old now?"

"Thirty- . . . two, and thirty-four."

"Grandchildren?"

"Yes."

He nodded, his eyes wandering off and focusing on his thoughts. Grandchildren. He had never even daydreamed grandchildren. His dreams had never gone beyond Randy. Then he looked up at her again, realized she was standing rather stiffly, watching. "Will you sit down?"

She didn't. "I don't like you being here, Stephen."

He was surprised. "Don't you want to hear . . . all of it?"

She thought, and found herself nodding. "Yes, I guess I do. But I'll tell you this: I think what you're doing is worse, worse than anything that was ever done to you, *or* to Randy."

There was strength in that, in the graceful stance of her slight body, in her eyes. He was surprised to see her so definite, and sad to see her so against him.

"It's the same. The same. Please sit down."

She sat across from him. He leaned forward, his words soft and carefully chosen. "I'm doing the same thing those five men did. It's all part of the same act." He gestured with his hands, teaching. "My actions are a reaction to *their* actions. It all fits together. Twenty years ago, they destroyed a very special life. Very special. *You* know. That kind of thing . . . it sets off vibrations. The vibrations don't diminish over time—they build. They are a signal that what happened isn't finished. It didn't end. The first act, the murder of Randy, was only half a thing. It was a question." He leaned even closer. "*I'm* the answer. Action—reaction. It's all a tight circle."

All that he said had been taken in and judged. He saw that, and he saw that he hadn't even begun to change her mind. She still stood against him. "*You* decided that," she said. "You created the circle—in your mind."

He shook his head. "No. It's there. How else could I do all this? How could Stephen Nye accomplish all these things and still be free? It's set up, Elaine. It's all fixed in place."

She was firm. "Oh. You heard a voice. A trumpet."

"Don't. Don't scoff like that. I felt the necessity of it. I was sure."

She drew in a shaky breath. She sighed. "It was ordained. You are the messenger of God."

His hands became fists that banged on his knees. "Not God. Not God. But there are forces—universal forces. Randy was *special*, you know . . ."

At Randy's name she closed her eyes and he saw her body stiffen with anger, more anger than he had ever seen in her. "Oh . . . God . . . *damn!* I hate . . . I hate what you're doing in the name of that poor boy." She leaned forward too. "Do not for one moment invoke the name of Randy! Randy is *not* part of what you're doing. You are not avenging Randy. You are just . . . striking out blindly. You just want to hurt because *you* were hurt. Not Randy. *You!* They took away your one friend. They released your prisoner. Yes! You were trying to imprison that boy, chain him to you. You wanted all of his time, his thoughts, his whole future. You wanted him for yourself. He was going to be your new life. Oh, yes! *That's* what they killed! Admit it! Admit it, and stop now. Stop before the last one. Stephen, at least let this one live!"

He sat back, his body slackened. He was surprised. He was hurt. "You knew him. You knew what he was. How can you say he wasn't special . . ."

"Oh, he was special. My God . . ." Tears came into her voice. "He was a loving, open child, and that's something we never were. That is something very special. Rare. A child with courage, born of two cowards, two beaten-down, meek people, *trained* to be meek people— Yes! He was special. But don't tell me you're going about the country leaving a trail of dead children because Randy was special! Don't tell me that! You are . . . wrong! You are just . . . one of the awful things about life. There are some ugly, terrible things about life, things like wars and torture and kidnapping and drunken drivers who can just . . . take an innocent life in one second, and stupid, shallow fraternity boys who hurt and kill without thinking. And you! You! Stephen Nye, you are just one of the ugly, terrible things now." She rested her elbows on her knees and dropped her face down into her hands. She didn't want to look at him anymore. "Get out of my house."

"You don't realize what's happened, Elaine."

She spoke without looking up. "Oh, I do. I do. You've murdered children . . . a man's wife. You've caused a suicide now, and you've . . . dirtied the memory of my son, *stained* it!"

She wasn't looking at him, didn't know what his reaction was. He spoke softly.

"I've brought him back."

Her face rose slowly from her hands. She stared at him a moment and whispered, "Oh, God."

Nye came forward, eager to explain, to share this with her. "He's alive again, at least in spirit. He's alive inside *me!*" He stood up in front of her. "Look at me. He's changing me. I'm younger, Elaine. I'm so much stronger. My mind, my body. I look people . . . in the face. I stare them down. I tell them, 'Get out of my way'—with my eyes, and they do! And I laugh . . . like he laughed. Elaine . . ." He bent his knees, came down to be eye level with her, inches away. "Even women . . . I want women again. Young women. That's Randy. Inside of me. That's what I've done. I've brought him back." He took her hands softly. "Elaine, I've brought him here to show you. Look at me. Look at Randy."

She was silently crying. She pulled her hands away and began to turn, but he held her shoulders.

"Look at him. Look at Randy!" He stood up suddenly, lifting her to her feet. "Look at him! Look!"

She pushed hard against his face, crying out. He stumbled back a step, surprised, staring wide-eyed as she screamed at him.

"No! You are not Randy!" She turned away, took a few aimless steps away, her hands covering her mouth. She fought through her tears and spoke with her back to him. "You're not Randy, and you're not Stephen. Not the one *I* knew." She stopped a moment, felt him come close to her, and she faced him. "I loved Stephen. He loved me. We had something . . . in our way. 'I won't hurt you if you don't hurt me.' We had that, anyway. Two weak people, holding on to each other. That wasn't bad, was it? How would you know? You weren't there. Stephen was there."

"I am Stephen. I am Randy. Together, I'm so strong now . . ."

"Yes, you're strong. You've . . . conquered your fears. Well, so have I. I didn't need to kill anyone to do it. Pain did it. And then love. My husband, his children. I'm different too. I can . . . talk to people, stand my ground, be proud of myself. It's too bad. It's too bad you shut me out. Maybe we could have grown together. It's too bad you never opened up to anyone, didn't fall in love, or at least . . . You were just so sick with anger. Stephen was. Not you. The sickness killed Stephen. Then *you* were born."

"I'm Randy."

"Stop it! You're a murderer, on his way to his next victim. Or is that me? Am I on your list, too?"

"Of course not, Elaine. I . . ."

"Why not? What's the difference? When you're the grim reaper, the great avenger . . ."

"I am Randy!"

"You are nobody! You are . . . a sickness!" She made a crisp turn and moved to the other side of the room, not hurrying, moving surely among her own things, her own reflection sliding along with her in a dozen vases and decanters and mirrors. She went to her desk, to her phone. She picked up the receiver and dialed. Nye started to walk toward her.

"Will you connect me with the police, please? Yes." Nye moved closer to her but didn't touch her. He reached out for the thin telephone cord. He looked at her, and his eyes were sad. He moved slowly, pulling at the cord until it ripped out of the wall. The phone was dead. She hung up and stared at him, met his eyes. Her voice had some of the tears left in it, but it was sure, clear.

"I'm going across the street. I'm going to call the police, and tell them that you're here." She waited. "Now what? Whoever you are . . . whatever you are, what do you do now? Stop me? Kill me? People are easy to kill. It doesn't take strength. It takes *weakness.* Emptiness." Tears now, sliding down. She didn't touch them. "There is nothing inside of you. No 'universal circles,' no Randy . . . no Stephen. Nothing." She started to move past him. "Do whatever you want."

She brushed by him, and she felt a tingle of fear, a chill on her neck. Her throat tightened, but she walked, she walked steadily to her door, sweeping her reflection along with her again. She opened the door and walked outside, didn't stop to look. She let it swing behind her. It closed with a soft click.

Stephen Nye found himself alone in another person's house. He stared at the door a moment, then looked about. He walked quietly, carefully, into the dining room and through it to the kitchen. He felt like a thief, an intruder. His eyes flicked about as he made his way. Someone's cookbooks. Someone's cup of coffee on the counter. Some stranger. He went to the door and opened it and went out.

15

"LOOK AT THE PELICANS."
The wave broke and poured over the sand, sloshing all the way to where Ellen sat, touching her bare heels and then drawing back.

"Won't you even look for a second at the goddamn pelicans?"

She leaned back on her hands, watching the birds fishing close to the shore. The day was suddenly darkened as a cloud reduced the sun to a perfect circle, pale yellow and harmless. Ellen could stare at it, study it. It was as cool as the moon.

Ellen was wearing a bikini, and she shivered. The next wave thumped heavily on the beach and surged forward, engulfing her feet, rushing up between her legs, chilling her. "It's ice water, Cross. There are icebergs out there. Look. Cross? Look at that big white whale. Look!"

Mr. Cross was sitting ten feet behind her like a lone, craggy boulder of the beach. His round body was covered by a baggy robe, and his balding head wobbled and turned like a loose stone upon the boulder. He sat with his back to Ellen and the ocean, and he moved his head constantly to scan the house, the cliffs, the trees, through a pair of binoculars.

"Cross, you're hopeless." Ellen moved to drier sand, sat with her legs curled under her, watching the sea again and waiting for the sun. "The Pacific is coming *alive* out there, and you're missing the whole show."

"Describe it," Cross said.

She lay on her stomach, her chin on her hands. "The water keeps changing color. The wind does it. And the sun. . . . Will you please turn around for one minute? Here. Give me the binoculars."

"No."

"Cross, you're making me nervous."

"I'm working, Ellen."

"You're just stubborn."

"This is my work." He always spoke slowly, gently. "This is what people buy when they hire me. I'm a watcher. I watch women's husbands, men's wives, stores' customers . . ."

"You're not watching anybody now. You're watching nothing."

He moved his head, moved his glance from the house to the cliffs to the trees, back again. "I'm watching everything."

She was quiet a moment, then she spoke with her chin moving on her hands. "I know it's harder for you when I'm out here. In the house you can relax."

"I like it out here."

"You do not, Cross. Your nose gets red, and you squint. You get headaches from squinting, and I'm sorry. Really. I just can't stay in the house anymore."

"Don't worry about it."

She sighed aloud and stood up, brushed the sand off her thighs and her stomach. "Cross, I never worry when you're around. You're my lifeguard. Do you swim?"

"No."

She laughed and saw that he was laughing too, silently, his round body shaking. She stood behind him and leaned over and kissed the very center of his bald head. He liked that. He smiled, but he didn't turn to her, and her mood darkened again.

"What are you looking for?" She burrowed with her toes into the sand until her leg ended at the ankle. "He's probably still in New York. He probably doesn't even *know* that guy shot himself. He might not know that. Even if he came here, where would he go? San Francisco? L.A.? He could never trace me here." In a moment her shoulders went slack. She sighed and drew her foot from the sand. "Shit. He's coming here right now. He's on his way." She sat down again and leaned against Cross's back.

"We don't know that."

"*I* know that." She hugged her knees. Far off, a fishing boat chugged along under its own storm cloud of gulls. The water changed from green to gray. "I can feel him coming for me. It's my turn."

"The police'll be ready. I'll be ready. We'll keep you safe."

She shrugged, and he felt her shrug against his back. "What're you supposed to do, Cross? It's my turn."

"We're supposed to catch him, and we will. He's just a man."

She put her chin on her knees. "He's not. He's not even a he."

"Oh? What is he?"

"He's one of the Furies. You know what the Furies are?"

"Tell me," Cross said, and he leaned back slightly. They supported each other. Two boulders on the beach.

"Greek spirits, Cross. Three of them. They live in the underground. Avenging spirits with long fingernails. Tangled hair. Alecto . . . Tisiphone . . ." Ellen suddenly stood and rubbed her arms, still watching the sea. "One of them has taken the shape of an old man, and she's been . . . on the loose, murdering the sons and the. . . . Now it's my turn."

"No it's not."

"Yes." She began moving to warm herself. She measured the distance and took one hopping step and did a cartwheel in the sand. She had been exercising to keep her legs strong and springy. She did a flip, this time without touching her hands to the ground. She landed lightly, gracefully, and adjusted her suit where it had moved a bit off the white patches of untanned skin. She stopped to get her breath. "You're facing the wrong way, Cross."

"Why?"

"Because this spirit isn't coming by any road. It's coming underground. It's down there right now, tunneling west, and it's going to keep moving until it hits salt water." She stepped to where the surf rushed up and cooled her feet. "Then it's going to surface, and it's going to be right out there, looking at me."

"Ellen . . . it's a man. Stephen Nye. Just a man."

"Sure. Then why won't you turn around, Cross? Even for one second to look at the pelicans."

He would have turned to glance at the birds then, but something moved. Some piece of the tableau of house and sand had been disturbed. He found the new shape, studied it.

"Your father."

Ellen turned and watched her father come walking across the sand, not hurrying, but coming briskly, down to business. He had a very straight-forward walk and a focused gaze. He had things to do, no time to waste. He seemed always to come at her that way. His purpose was to put things in order. He would arrange her life, give orders, make suggestions. Then he would leave. He was close enough now so that she could see his familiar frown. He usually frowned upon arrival in her life, frowned at the disorder he saw. He seemed to want to straighten this beach, bury the dark tangles of seaweed, smooth the sand.

She thought again how handsome he was, neat and rugged with a good strong jaw. My father's a doll, she would still say to a new friend. He used to be a pilot.

The pilot had landed in her life again, already

eager for take-off. She was an island he visited. It came to her now, on this beach, that she was an island visited by everyone in her life, visited and left. She longed to be landlocked, surrounded by and connected to people who stayed, people who held on.

"Well, here we go," the pilot said, and she wished his next words would be, "The plane is ready. Get your gear. We fly in ten minutes." But he said, "They spotted Nye in Springfield, Illinois. They know he's on his way here. Plans have changed."

Conversations began quietly, indirectly. A dozen subjects were touched gently, like eggs, examined briefly and put away, the shells never broken. Ellen's mother watched half of a tennis game on television. Frank and Mr. Cross had drinks. Ellen looked through a magazine. Dora served a snack. There was no energy, no focus. They were only waiting. The police were due at four. It was three-fifteen. Mr. Cross sat beside his packed suitcase. He was leaving. Plans had changed.

Frank swished the ice around in his glass, spoke to his drink. "Cops are finally . . . getting on the stick. All this time and now they . . ." He let it trail off, finished the drink.

"Well . . . he wasn't L.A.'s responsibility." Cross sipped at a gin and tonic that he didn't want. The movement of glass to lips was something to do to help the time go by. "Until now."

Ellen's mother was staring at her slacks, picking at tiny specks of lint. "Maybe we should go away."

Frank went to the bar to make another drink. "I can't go away. Maybe you and Ellen."

"We could send Ellen to Mexico," her mother said to the lint.

"For how long?" Frank turned to Cross. "How long you think it'll take?"

"What?"

"To catch him."

Ellen looked up from her magazine, looked at Cross fumbling for words and then shrugging. Her father had asked a stupid question. It showed he knew nothing about Stephen Nye and what sort of a thing Stephen Nye was to deal with. Cross knew. He only shrugged. Ellen's mother gave up against the lint. She sighed. "Of course, the Groffs went away."

There was silent acknowledgment. The men sipped their drinks. "Why does Cross have to go?" Ellen said.

"The cops are taking over the whole show."

"So?"

"So . . ." Her father shrugged. "So we're going to have round-the-clock protection. Like we should've had from the start. Free."

Free. The word reminded Ellen that Cross was being paid for every minute he spent with her. Her lifeguard came high, by the hour, day, or week. "Oh," she said, and there was some loss in her voice. Old Santa Claus, old kindly Cross, was a gigolo. But Frank Skate read his daughter's answer another way.

"You think it's the money?"

"Oh, Dad . . ."

"You think I'd be cheap in a situation like this? With your life . . ."

"Dad, of course not."

"It's the *job* of the cops to do this." He gulped his drink and swished the ice about, defensive, scared.

The wall was crushing him, driving him into the ground.

Ellen's mother checked the time, spoke to her watch. "Ellen, please change."

Ellen had put on cut-off jeans, and still wore her bikini top. "Change?"

"Put something on top."

"You think two weeks would do it?" Frank said. "Cross? Two weeks?"

The older man was puzzled. "For what?"

"For Ellen in Mexico."

Cross looked at Ellen and she turned away, embarrassed for her father. Cross shrugged. "Can't tell."

"Can't tell." Frank shook his head, sipped his drink. His wife had caught the signal. So had Ellen. He had repeated Cross's last words with an edge of hostility in his voice. The gin was starting to tell. "God . . . damn. This kid says, 'Let's go get one of the pledges and take him up into the woods,' and here we are, *sitting* here. . . . Because that stupid kid said that. And that stupid Randy Nye, hanging around, willing. Just . . . so . . . *happy* to be the one. Why didn't he pick another fraternity. Why didn't he have the fucking flu that night."

"Oh, Frank."

"Oh, Frank." He drained his glass. She tried to change the subject.

"How many police are coming?"

"What? I don't know. One from Chicago."

Ellen's mother gave her classic look of mild surprise. "Why Chicago?"

"Why? I don't know. They'll be here. Ask them."

Ellen watched her parents, saw how they avoided

each other's eyes, how their looks went out through windows or turned inward to their thoughts. They were where they didn't want to be. Ellen had always felt that. Home was a place her parents ran from. She imagined how they must change when they left, how they must sigh and smile to be away from each other and from home and from her. She pulled on the embroidered shirt she had laid across her lap. But her mother didn't see her, didn't look away from the window as she said, "Ellen, are you just going to sit there like that?" And her father didn't take his eyes off the glass he was sliding from hand to hand when he said, "She's all set to . . . wow the cops when they come in."

Cross looked at his drink, embarrassed. Ellen, leaned back hard in the chair, looked at the ceiling.

"Christ, why don't *you* two leave? Why don't *you* go to Mexico until it's over? Take a month. It'll be over in a month, one way or another. Right? Cross?"

Frank said, "Don't be silly." And Ellen's mother spoke without turning from her window. "We'll just wait to see what the police say."

"The police." Frank laughed a bitter laugh. "The police were supposed to take care of it months ago. A problem comes up, you should be able to put it into somebody's hands and have them take care of it. It never works that way. It's never clean. There's always something. You trust somebody to sell some real estate, and they fuck it up. You trust somebody to catch a criminal, a murderer. You trust somebody to build a simple bonfire!" His voice broke, "Jesus! All of this because Groff fucked up the fire. Why didn't he stop with Groff? Groff was the one. What did I do?"

Ellen remembered and spoke to the ceiling, not answering her father, just suddenly remembering. "The handcuffs."

Frank looked at her, came toward her, stiff and pale.

Ellen's mother said, "What? What handcuffs?"

But Frank went to Ellen and leaned close to her. He slowly put out a hand that gripped her shoulder. "Listen." His fingers hurt her.

"What handcuffs?" her mother said. But Frank still ignored her, spoke slowly, carefully, to Ellen, squeezing her shoulder in cadence with his words.

"Listen, the cuffs didn't kill him, did they?"

"No, I just . . ."

"The fire killed him, right?"

"Right."

"Groff killed him." He let go of her shoulder, but his eyes still held her. "Groff was the one responsible, and he knew it. Why do you think he shot himself?"

Ellen met his stare, her own eyes beginning to fill with tears. How the pilot hated her, look at him hating her, look at his eyes. "Dad . . ."

"I know you wish *I* would do that." He turned and walked away from her, his voice shaky. "I'm supposed to solve it for you. I'm supposed to end it. That's what you hope."

"Dad . . . no!"

Frank spoke to Cross, "She does," and to his wife, "I know she does." Ellen was crying.

"No, Daddy, Jesus . . ."

Ellen's mother had turned from the window to stare at her husband, now she looked back at the view of the beach, spoke to the beach. "Frank, for God's sake."

"For God's sake," he mimicked.

Ellen stood and walked around her chair, heading out of the room, passing Mr. Cross, who looked at the rug. She went into her room and closed the door. She sat on the bed and listened. She could hear her parents, but couldn't make out the words. It was the familiar sound of the house again, the sound of all the houses she had lived in with her parents. She knew now it wasn't their voices she heard. That murmuring through the walls, those sharp shouts and hisses and the mean mocking laughter—these were the sounds of their spirits going mad as they battered against doors and windows and walls trying to get away from each other, from home, from her.

The police arrived at five. Ellen's mother hurried to Ellen's room and shouted through the door, then hurried back to greet the three officers. The two who stood talking to her husband and Mr. Cross were tall men, trim and neat. There was a shorter one who stayed near the door and searched the room with his eyes, searched her and made her uncomfortable. He was not as all-in-place as the others. The lines of his face, hair, and clothes were roughly scribbled and he moved too much—moved his shoulders, moved his head, moved his eyes around the room.

Dela nodded to the Skates and Mr. Cross when he was introduced, then he went back to checking the room, the windows, the beach outside. He flexed his back, his shoulders, stepped about restlessly. His restlessness had grown over the past month. Dela was a hitter, ready with a punch, a fast combination of blows. He was a boxer stalking an empty ring. He wanted to hit that man. He wanted to stop him. Every muscle in his back and arms and shoulders and hands was springy and ready and aching to punch Stephen Nye.

He turned to Mrs. Skate. "Where is your daughter?"

"I'll get her." But in a few minutes she came back into the room alone, angry, embarrassed. She spoke to her husband. "*You* try to get her out of there."

"What?"

"She won't come out and she won't let me in."

Frank laughed a strange laugh of disbelief. "She what?" He went off to Ellen's room. Mrs. Skate smiled at the police, an empty smile they didn't return.

Dela spoke. "She's locked in her room?"

"Yes."

They heard Frank knocking. "Ellen?"

Dela went to him, the other cops followed leisurely, speaking to Mr. Cross. Frank turned to Dela, but didn't look at him. His eyes looked off, focused on his anger. He said, "Bitch," under his breath.

Dela asked how long she'd been in there, but Frank ignored him, knocked again. Mrs. Skate answered. "An hour ago she just . . . went into her room. Mad, I guess. Ellen, please!"

"She say anything?" Dela looked at Frank, his wife. "You sure she's in there?"

"She's in there. Ellen, what're you doing?!"

Dela stared at that door. The others were speaking to each other, to Ellen, but Dela only stared. Behind that white wooden door his fear slowly revolved, showing its faces—Mrs. King's dead and bloodied face in the elevator, Daniel King shaking his head no, trying to keep her alive by not accepting her death, and Pegi Stanton next, her eyes full of memories and terror, her face slowly revolving, turning away as the face of Donny Groff appeared. Dela saw the boy's wide-eyed shock as he looked into his father's room. In his mind, Dela heard the shotgun go off again. He heard Mrs. Groff's long and painful scream, and he kicked at that door with all his strength. It loosened but didn't give. His kick shocked and silenced the others. He poised for another try.

"What are you doing?"

"Don't break the . . ."

He kicked again. The lock was tearing through the frame. One of the L.A. cops said, "Hey, Dela . . ." and Mrs. Skate put her hands to her cheeks. "Don't!" Frank took his arm, but Dela pulled away and kicked again, and the door smashed open.

He looked for blood, for a corpse. He sent his eyes flying about the room, searching for what he didn't want to find. The room was empty. The window was open.

Ellen turned away from the road as a truck blew past. It hummed out of sight, and the silence settled back around her. She shuffled a foot on the loose stones on the side of the road, but that small sound only magnified the silence, gave it a shape and a weight that bore down on her. She raised a thumb to an oncoming station wagon. The wagon sang by, the people inside immobile, blank faces staring straight ahead. She had a feeling about the next car, a black Volkswagen, one man inside. The car slowed. She knew it would stop, and it did. She opened the door and slid into the seat. "Thanks." She studied the man as he turned to check the road. He was middle-aged, maybe older. He was tall.

He glanced at her and smiled a small smile of greeting. She looked at his eyes.

"Are you him?" she said.

"What?"

"I thought you might be him."

"Who?"

She rested back against the seat. "Doesn't matter. I guess I'm going to L.A."

16

AL LENZ used the hose like a machine gun, blasting at bits of dirt and grass blades on the sidewalk. He spotted a bug and strafed it, moving the hose slowly, bringing the explosions of water closer and closer behind the panicky beetle. He made the sound of gunfire in his mind, closing the gap between his bullets and his running target. The water engulfed the bug and erased it.

"Hi there."

Lenz turned to see a man standing in the center of the yard, smiling at him. The wet grass was up over the man's shoes, but he didn't seem to mind. He waved.

Lenz crimped the hose to stop the flow. The plastic bulged in his hand, the water hissing there, threatening. "Hello."

The man waved toward the apartment building. "You the manager?"

"Yes. No vacancies, though."

The man nodded and pointed a shoe at the sign in the yard, touched the sign with the toe of his shoe just where it read, FRANK SKATE REALTY. "Thinking of buying it."

"Oh. Well, you should call Mr. Skate, make an appointment."

The man nodded, put his hands on his hips, looking over the building. "I know Skate. We've talked about this property, drove by here together." He grinned. "He's quite a salesman, isn't he. You know him?"

"I've met him."

"Nice man."

"Yes."

"He's going to show me the place Sunday."

"Oh."

"Nice neighborhood, isn't it?"

Lenz agreed, following the man's glance up and down the block. The man turned to him, smiling again. "Yeah, I'll be out here Sunday with Skate and his wife. You know his wife?"

Lenz shrugged. "Never met her."

"I think he's got some kids."

"Got a daughter at UCLA," Lenz said.

"Mm." The man nodded as he looked over the building, then he gave a wave and walked off. "Thanks."

"Sure," Lenz said. He watched the man a moment, wondering what it was that seemed odd about him. His moves, he decided. He was a man of fifty-five or so, maybe older, but his moves were much younger, his walk, his wave. They were almost boyish.

Ellen stayed in a Holiday Inn in Hollywood for three days, ordering food in her room and sleeping in her clothes. She couldn't decide where to go. Any time she had ever traveled it had always been *with* someone or *to* someone. She didn't want to go to people. Not this time. Not anymore. She would stay alone, move alone through new cities and sunny stucco countries until she collided with a sure friend.

She made lists of places. She made lists of jobs she could do. She watched television all night and slept until noon and never left the motel. She realized that any time she had ever been alone, she had made lists and stayed up all night watching television so she wouldn't have to think. Being Ellen Skate and being alone didn't go together. She decided she wouldn't be Ellen Skate anymore.

She took a shower and washed her hair with hand soap. She threw away her dirty underwear and put on her clothes only long enough to get her to a store. She bought an outfit that Ellen Skate would not have bought—tall boots and gaucho pants, a loose, fancy blouse, sash belt. In the mirror she saw a little pirate girl. She stood with her legs apart and her hands on her hips and she smiled.

She didn't buy underwear, just put the clean clothes on her clean body and left her dirty things behind. She paid for the clothes and the room with her parents' credit cards. She went to a bank and got an advance of five hundred dollars with one of the cards. Then she broke the cards in half and threw them away, cleaned out her wallet and threw Ellen Skate away. Someday she would send her parents the money, send it from Bolivia or a Caribbean Island, a pirate's island. She called herself Kathleen, Kathleen Orista, but no one asked her name.

Stephen Nye swam in a sea of young faces, young bodies. He passed close to them, moved through the air they stirred, smelled their scents, heard the broken bits of conversation that trailed them: "A midterm last . . . didn't hear me . . . cut the class three . . . God I *hope* so . . . this weekend . . . *Ulysses* . . . "

He did a bouncy trot down the stairs to the lower floor of the library, where the phones were. All the booths were full. He waited. He leaned back against the wall and drummed on the cool stone with the palms of his hands. He nodded to a girl who had come to stand nearby, and they smiled briefly, sharing for a moment the bond of waiting. A boy finished his call, and Nye went into the booth, dialed.

"UCLA information."

"Hi. Does the university publish a student directory?"

"Are you trying to locate a student?"

"Yes."

"Call Student Information, eight-two-five, four-six-seven-one."

"Thank you."

"Student Information."

"Hi. Is there a directory of students?"

"No, but we have the information here if you're looking for someone."

"Yes. A student named Ellen Skate. S-k-a-t-e."

"One moment."

"Is she currently registered?"

"I'm not sure."

"One moment."

"Ellen Skate. Yes, I have her on the list for last term, but not the current quarter."

"Can you give me the address?"

"Yes, it's Eight-two-four . . . Hillman Street. Phone number, seven-four-one . . . o-nine-nine-o."

"O-nine-nine-o. . . . Thank you. Thanks a lot."

"You're welcome."

"Bye."

"Goodbye."

Ellen wandered the city in new boots, walking slowly, enjoying the sun. Her purse seemed pounds lighter. There was nothing in it but make-up and money, no identity. She would have to start collecting a new one, gathering all the ticket stubs and year-old receipts, out-of-date library cards and forgotten keys. She hadn't picked a new town yet. Somewhere warm.

Arizona. Flagstaff? Take a bus. She heard a bus hissing to a stop half a block away. It was only a city bus, plodding from corner to corner, but it was a beginning. She'd be off the ground, on wheels, in motion. She ran for the bus.

She sat and watched the store windows blur together as the bus strained and roared toward the next stop. She made lists in her mind. Flagstaff. Cold in the winter. Snow. Tall trees. Pretty country but cold. Maybe Phoenix. Too hot. Social Security card in the name of Kathleen Orista. Irish-Spanish. Black-Irish and Basque. Kathleen Inez Orista.

The bus stopped, started, turned. She didn't notice. People sat next to her, left. Only one spoke.

"Hello."

He was a bent-over old man, bent almost to breaking. He sat stiffly, leaning forward and turning to smile at her.

She said, "Hello," but it was barely above a whisper. She was staring at his eyes. They seemed to know her.

"Pretty day."

She nodded, staring. The bent back was a disguise. The face was altered, hair was whitened. This was a tall man, a tall straight man whose eyes were laughing at her, knowing her. She was sure. It was him.

"Going home or to work?"

"Home," she whispered.

He nodded, and for a time he looked straight ahead into the back of the next seat. Then he twisted about to see her again, and he smiled again. "I'm heading home too. What's your name?"

She only stared. She swallowed, whispered. "Ellen." Because he knew. He knew anyway.

He began to move, to stand, and she was sure he

would straighten up now. He would be as tall as the top of the bus. He would reach out to touch her, and out of his sleeve would come the curled talon of a Fury. She would scream and die.

"This is my stop, Ellen." He rose awkwardly, still bent nearly in half. He shuffled to the door and left the bus.

She watched him cross the street. She was tight and shaking inside. Stephen Nye was close to her. He was in the eyes of that old man. He was real and he was in this city.

The bus pulled away, and she noticed which street she was on, which way she was moving. This was a Wilshire bus, heading west. She would get off at UCLA and talk to somebody she knew, talk to Ann, just for a while. She needed to.

She leaned back in the seat and took a breath, closed her eyes. She was going to people.

Some of them pumped up and down as they walked, some shuffled. There were tall, long striders and others with quick, short steps. A few of them jogged and some of them strolled slowly, chattering to each other. They were men and women from eighteen to thirty-five or so, each moving in his own rhythm, but all of them going to or coming from the UCLA campus. Ellen's street was a two-way river of students and professors all day long. Some of them lived nearby. Others drove in and parked early in the morning, returning to their cars between classes to study and eat and even nap.

Stephen Nye walked openly down this street, a long

strider in desert boots and worn clothes, an outdoor man, tough, even brazen in his walk, wearing hair long enough to curl out from under his knit cap. His mustache was flamboyant, his necklace of shells a badge, his whole manner a challenge.

He carried a book, slapping it against his thigh as he walked. He looked into everyone's eyes and into the parked and passing cars. *Look at me.* He chanted to the slapping of the book. *Look at me. Look at me.* He feared no one. *Look at me.* The fugitive, Stephen Nye, was safely hidden inside the most conspicuous man on the street. *Look at me.*

He approached an old camper with a scratched and faded painting of a sunset on its side. He climbed in and leaned far back in the seat, getting comfortable, opening his book. He was parked across from Ellen's building, watching the entrance. He had already phoned her and gotten no answer. He had already been in the open entrance-way where the mailboxes were. Her name was still on the box: A. BYNUM/E. SKATE.

He was watching that mailbox now. He had sent Ellen a letter, just an envelope stuffed with blank paper. He was hoping someone would open the box and write a forwarding address on the envelope, then place it on the shelf above the boxes where he could grab it. It could happen that way. It could even happen that she herself would collect her mail, that she was still living at this address, that right now she was inside the apartment just yards away from him, sitting in a chair, lying in bed, looking out the window, her life just yards away from his hands.

He crossed his legs at the ankles, moved his tennis

shoes from side to side, watched all the women who passed near or through that entrance-way.

You. You be the one. You go to that mailbox. You be her. You with the maroon dress. Oh, I'll go under that dress. My hands, my fingers will go fast, go under the cloth to your skin and touch you with torches. You'll burn and scream. You. You be her.

She wouldn't let Ann call her parents. She would make Ann promise not to call even after she left. But Ann would call anyway. All right. She'd ask Ann to call them one hour after she had gone. "Call them and tell them I'm fine," Ellen said in her mind. "I'm traveling the world. I'm okay. He'll never find me. Tell them they can just . . . go back to their lives." Ann would argue with her. Ellen had to be absolutely firm. She wouldn't let Ann talk her into anything. She wouldn't let Ann turn her into Ellen Skate again. She was through with Ellen Skate. She was just one block from the apartment.

She remembered some of these faces, others were new. A few of the cars were familiar too. There was a couple in the back seat of one car, mouths open, eyes closed, laughing soundlessly behind the glass, weaving, limp with laughter. They collapsed out of sight.

She nearly laughed aloud, sharing their pleasure for a moment, imagining herself in the back seat of a car, laughing with a lover as, outside, a girl walked by. She wouldn't see that girl. She would be holding tight to her lover, her eyes closed with laughter, and the girl outside would not exist.

Ellen felt herself disappearing as she walked by the

car. Her body dissolved. The wind blew through her as through smoke. She drifted to her building like a ghost, and reached out to touch something, to see if she were there.

She had her hand on her mailbox. A. BYNUM/E. SKATE. There was mail inside. She opened her purse, then remembered she had thrown away the keys. She swore and tried the box—locked. It was probably all for Ann, probably junk, but she liked collecting the mail. She liked the possibilities. She enjoyed the act of opening the box and flipping through the envelopes. It was the same as picking up a poker hand to see what had been dealt to her. Within the moment of picking up the cards, all the possibilities are suspended. Four aces. Royal flush. Letter from a friend. Letter from home. She jiggled the box once more, then left it, trotted up the metal stairs. If Ann wasn't home, she would wait, sit outside a while, or maybe she would go to the campus.

She walked to the door, imagining Ann's face, her surprise. The doorbell was in the center of the door, but even as she reached for it, she noticed that the door was slightly open, still in the frame, but pushed back from the lock. She readied herself and hit the door with the flat of her hand, swinging it wide. She stepped inside and stood there with her hands on her hips, smiling toward the kitchen. "Hey! Guess who it is?"

Behind her, a man's voice said, "Ellen?"

She whirled around, already stepping backward, losing her balance and crashing into a lamp, stumbling back against the wall.

"Ellen Skate?"

Dela stared at the girl who was trying to disappear into the wall, her big eyes so afraid of him. He was sure now. He had studied the photos and this was Ellen Skate. Deep in his mind, an alarm bell stopped ringing. It had rung for days, ever since he had broken into her room and found it empty. The bell had started then, jangling inside of him—she's gone. She's out there. He can find her. He can finish her. You can't stop him. She's out there. The bell stopped and he drew in a long breath. She's here with me. I can see her, touch her. If he wants her now, he has to come to me. To me.

He was already moving when he spoke, holstering his revolver, swinging the door closed. "It's okay, I'm a police officer." He turned back to her, and she hadn't moved. He showed her his shield. "Jim Dela, Chicago Police Department." Her eyes went from the shield to his face, then they filled with tears and she walked away from him, sat down, not looking at him.

"You all right?"

She didn't speak for a moment. Then the words bubbled out. "Jesus *Christ*! I really thought it was him. I thought you were him . . . disguised younger, y' know . . . and shorter. I thought, He's got me. This is it. Christ. I thought you were going to *shoot*." She looked at him. "If a bullet kills you, do you hear the shot?"

He shrugged, but she was already going on.

"I think my heart . . . I think I was dead for half a

second at least. You almost killed me from shock. That can happen. Why did you *do* that?"

"Sorry."

She flopped her head back on the sofa cushions, closed her eyes. "What are you doing here anyway? Where's Ann?"

"I'm waiting here." He moved to a window that overlooked the courtyard and he glanced outside for the five-hundredth time. "We moved her out. Somebody called the school for your address. Probably Nye." She was silent, getting her breath. He watched her. She was slouched down on the sofa, her legs spread, boot heels on the floor. Her stomach rose and fell with quick breaths. She was trim and pretty and looking like some kind of musketeer in that outfit, D'Artagnan, Puss 'n Boots. "Your parents are going nuts."

She opened her eyes and looked at the ceiling a moment, thoughtful, sad. "Look, I'll just go now, okay?"

"What d' you mean, 'just go'?"

"Away."

"Away?"

"Away! I'm not going home. I'm just going. I'm *gone* as far as you're concerned. I'm gone for good. I've disappeared. I'm not even here." Her outburst had brought her to the edge of the sofa. Now she sat back and crossed her legs, one boot swinging above the floor.

He studied her, sat next to her. "You're not even here."

"Right."

He paused. "Where are you?"

"Nobody knows."

He nodded a moment. "Where are you going?"

"Everyplace."

"Why?"

"So he can't find me. So my parents can just forget about me. So my father can go to Canada and fly airplanes and my mother can have all the 'guests' she wants sleeping over, and everybody will be just fine. Fine. Except Nye. He'll be miserable. He'll spend the rest of his life trying to catch up to me and he never will. He'll die of old age. Everybody's happy."

Dela studied her a moment, and she met his eyes. "But they're not happy. They're going nuts."

"They're going through the *motions* of going nuts because that's what everybody expects. Inside they're sighing a big sigh of relief. She's finally gone. My God, I thought that girl would *never* leave. Sure, they're worried, but I'll write them a letter just as I leave this town. They'll get it tomorrow. I'll explain everything, and then I'll be finished explaining, finished for good, finished being Ellen Skate."

She leaned back and put her feet up on the coffee table. In a moment he did the same. She spoke without looking at him. "Aren't you going to ask me who I am now?"

"Who?"

"Kathleen Orista."

He stared.

"Kathleen Inez Orista."

He just looked, then he said, "How do you know that Nye isn't standing outside that goddamn door right now? What makes you think you can stay ahead of him?"

"All I have to do is stop being Ellen Skate—that's all."

"There are four dead people—four. They couldn't stay ahead of him or hide from . . ."

She broke in, angry. "You don't have to tell me about Nye. I know what he is, better than anybody. I know that he doesn't travel on airplanes, never needs to eat or sleep. He's always awake and always with a different face. He's a Fury and there is no way for policemen or guards or dogs to stop him. I will not wait for him. I will not sit between those two people who hate each other and sit and wait and wait and watch them hate each other and hate me . . ." There were tears in her voice now. "I will not depend on anyone to protect me. I'm just going to run out into the world and completely disappear!" She put a hand to her face and turned away from him.

He waited a moment before he spoke. "I can't let you."

"What?"

"I can't let you disappear."

"You can't stop me."

"Ellen . . . you and me have to stick close, very close. Until we catch Nye or kill him, you and me are just inches away from each other. . . . Hey. Don't."

She was up and moving to the door, not rushing, almost marching to that door. He went after her, and then she ran.

"Don't open . . ." but her hand was on the knob and she was swinging the door wide. He grabbed her from behind, throwing an arm around her waist and pulling her back against him as his other hand pushed at the door, pushing it out of her grip. She kicked and twisted against him. He held her with both arms and slammed his back into the door. It closed, and he went with it, losing his balance. He was holding her off the floor, one arm around her waist, the other circling her chest. She squirmed and kicked backward. A boot heel hit his shin, and he let her go. She whirled around to face him, flushed and panting. He held out a hand toward her, a warning hand. "Go sit down." Then, just as she was about to speak, he shouted it, "Go sit down!"

She walked away from him, walked across the room and turned to stare at him, hands on her hips, her eyes cursing him. She was still breathing heavily, her mouth open. Her blouse had come out of her waistband, and she tucked it back in, watching him.

He limped to a chair. "Goddamn son of a *bitch*." He sat on the arm of the chair and rubbed his shin. "Take off those boots."

She pushed a hand through her hair, angry and embarrassed from the struggle. "You can't keep me here, you know."

"Take off the boots now. Or I'll take 'em off you."

"You have no right to keep me here!"

"You're a runaway!"

"I'm eighteen!"

"You're in protective custody!"

"Bull*shit*!"

"*Take off those fucking boots!*"

She stared at him, then she sat down and leaned back in the sofa, raised a foot off the floor, raised a boot for him to take off.

Their eyes were locked on each other, and she was defiant. He stood up and came toward her, still favoring his leg. He grabbed her boot heel and raised it up high, nearly pulling her off the sofa. He kept his eyes on her as he unzipped the boot and yanked it off.

"Ouch. Goddamn it!"

He dropped the boot and waited. Her stare was burning him. She raised the other boot. He unzipped it. This time she pulled her own foot out. She tucked her legs under her and moved back on the sofa. He dropped the second boot, still watching her and just now remembering how she had felt in his arms, only now becoming aware of how good her breasts had felt under that thin silky blouse. The memory aroused him without denting his anger. "Now you don't move from there."

"Or you shoot."

He went to the phone and picked it up, glancing at her. Her face changed as he dialed. She became afraid. "I won't go home." Then, "Please!"

"Raye. . . . This is Dela."

"Shit." She turned away from him.

"What kind of surveillance you got on my street out here? . . . Yeah? Well, they should stop and park and move around. They're undercover aren't they? It's all students here. They stopping people? . . . Uh-huh. He could be a woman. He could be a goddamn telephone pole, you know. : . . Yeah. Okay. . . . No word? Mm. Bye." He hung up and looked at her. She turned to him, wondering.

"You didn't say I was here."

He put his weight on his leg and swore and limped about.

"Why didn't you?"

He sat and pulled up his pants leg, inspecting the redness on his shin. It was swelling a bit. "Look at that. Jesus."

"Are you going to let me go?"

He spoke as he examined his wound. "We'll see."

"It's the best thing for everybody. Really."

The best thing, Dela thought, the very best thing, would be a knock at the door. He'd have Ellen there to answer. She'd say, "Yes." And Nye would probably say, "Police." Then Dela would get ready. He would hide the girl and open the door and shoot Nye's eyes out. That would be the best thing. And it *could* happen that way. It just might happen, because there she was, sitting across the room from him, Nye's intended.

He would play it this way for a while. He would give Nye time to trace her, to make his move. He would not tell Sergeant Raye. He did *not* want her to be swept away by the L.A.P.D. and sent out of town. That would muddy things, stretch things out. This way it was so simple. It was almost as if Dela were back in Chicago, waiting in Nye's hotel room, waiting for him to come. That's where it should have ended. This was Dela's second chance. It would end here.

"I'll write my parents and tell them I'm fine. I'm traveling around the world. They can just go back to their lives now. Okay? When the cops see that letter they'll call off the case, right? It's over for everybody."

"We'll see."

"You keep saying . . ."

"We'll see! Now, so far I haven't told anybody. I should have, but I didn't. Don't make me change my mind. I want to . . . get a feeling, get a line on where Nye is. They'll probably spot him soon, pick up a trace. . . . Then, when I think it's safe, I'll open the door for you, all right? I'll turn my back."

"All right. Yes! Thanks."

If Nye didn't knock on their door in two days, Dela would turn her over to the cops, to her parents. He was buying time with her. He felt he only needed a little time. The knock would come.

"How did you get here?"

"Took a bus to UCLA and walked."

"See anybody who . . ."

"Who was tall and old with . . . nice straight features and gray hair at the temples? Sure. Every time I blink."

"Anybody know you're in town?"

"No. Except if *he* knows."

Dela nodded, thought a moment. "Can I trust you not to run? If you run out of here, I call the cops—and we've got you back with your parents so fast . . ."

"Yes! Trust me not to run."

He stood up. "I want to hear you. Keep talking."

"What?"

"I have to go to the john. I want to know you're still out here, so talk."

She laughed and kept laughing, giddy with relief because she wasn't going home.

He shook his head, walked to the bathroom, and went in.

She stopped laughing. "What should I say?" She laughed again. "What should I talk about? This is really. . . . Can you hear me in there? I can hear you.

Why don't you run the water or something? Should I sing?"

Kathleen Orista opened the door to the closet that once was Ellen Skate's. She saw the clothes that Ellen had left behind, the odd blouses that matched nothing, the fancy dresses, the old, crinkled dancing shoes. She touched the garments and remembered, felt a long cloth coat and thought of San Francisco, saw and smelled chilly San Francisco. She drew a hand across the limp dresses, and out flew images of weddings, formal dances, good-night embraces. A scarf dangled down from a hanger. A yellow woven cap was bunched on the edge of the shelf. There were other things far back on that shelf that she couldn't see, that she would never see again. They were already out of her life. She was already far away.

There was a full-length mirror on the closet door. She looked into it and spoke absently, sending her voice to the kitchen where she could hear Dela moving about. "I'm going to do my hair blond. And I'll pick a new name because Orista doesn't. . . . Well I guess it *could*. Aren't some Spanish people blond?"

"You hungry?"

"If you are." She knelt and rummaged on the floor, found a shoebox full of half-pencils and dry pens and her address book. She picked up the book.

"I could fry some eggs."

"No." She tossed the book back into the shoebox. "Let's call for a pizza." She went into the kitchen. Dela was opening the phonebook. "*I'll* call. The number's by the phone." She went to the phone and looked closely at the wall. She had written phone numbers there in pencil and Ann had washed them off. She had used ink for the pizza number. It was still readable. She dialed. "What kind?"

"Plain."

"Plain?"

"Plain."

"I'll get half plain. A medium?"

"Large."

Dela had finished his half of the pizza and was eating from Ellen's side. She slouched back and put her feet up on the chair opposite her. "I was in Chicago."

"Oh yeah?"

She nodded. "When I was . . . about twelve. For a week I think. There's some big fountain there."

"Buckingham Fountain."

"Yeah. It lights up."

"Right."

"I was there, and I remember State Street. That's the big one, right?"

"Michigan Avenue is bigger . . . cleaner."

"We stayed at the Edgewater Beach Hotel."

"They tore it down."

"Yeah?"

"Yeah, I live near there."

"No kidding? We were probably close to each other . . . six years ago."

He nodded, eating. Then he stopped and stared at her. "Six years ago you were *twelve*?"

"Yeah."

"Jesus."

"How old were *you?*"

"Twenty-six."

"Christ."

They both raised their glasses of ice water and drank and brought them down on the table top almost in unison. She looked at him a while.

"Cold in Chicago."

He nodded.

"I was thinking of going someplace warmer, but I could see Chicago a while." She glanced at him as she said it, a wondering, testing glance. He nodded. "I could stop by your place." Her mind rushed ahead, flashing pictures of Chicago, of herself knocking on Dela's door, of Dela opening the door, and both of them smiling. She glanced again. He was busy eating. "Will you give me the address?"

"Sure."

"Maybe you could help me find a job."

"Mm. What kind?"

"I'm a dancer. Not really professional, but I've performed a lot—local groups, musicals . . ."

"Ballet dancer?"

"Some. Mostly modern."

"Mm."

"You dance?"

"Me?"

She laughed at his amazed expression. "You said you weren't married. You must take girls out. You must go dancing once in a while."

"Well, yeah, but that's . . ."

"That's modern dance."

"It's just . . ."

"It's modern dance. You hear the rhythm, and you move to it, right?"

"I don't go much."

"I love dancing. 'Heart, have no pity on this house of bone: shake it with dancing.'" He looked at her, and she flushed a little. "Edna St. Vincent Millay wrote that." She had never quoted it before. "I really love it. When the music starts, it fills me up. It's a transfusion. I've got music all through me instead of blood, and I'm moving to the heartbeat of the drums. *I* made that up."

He put his elbows on the table, thoughtful. "You know what I like?"

"What?"

"You don't see it much anymore."

"What?"

"Except in old movies."

"*What?*"

"Tap dancing."

"Oh, I tap."

"Somebody like Fred Astaire or Gene Kelly. Remember how they would smile?" Now *he* was a bit embarrassed, exposing this private fancy. "They'd start to dance and they'd smile . . ." He shook his head, remembering.

"Dela."

"What?"

"I'll tap for you. Can I put my boots on? Wait!" She was up, gone. "I've got tap shoes in the closet! Did Ann leave the radio?"

"No."

"Hum something. Ready?"

He smiled to himself, to the empty room, an embarrassed smile. "Hey, I can't hum."

He hummed a few bars of "Tea for Two" in a very small voice, trying it out. The signals went up, the sirens. They stopped him—the old signals that always pulled him back when he was about to plunge over an edge. You're being a fool, the signals warned. Don't be a fool. He stopped humming. "Hey, I can't."

"Ready?"

"I'm not humming."

She hummed. She came dancing into the kitchen in tap shoes, humming "Yankee Doodle Dandy," and he sat at the table, feeling foolish. He kept his eyes on her feet at first, not really watching. He was uncomfortable. She was making him uncomfortable, and so he resented her. He raised his eyes to her body. His stare attacked her breasts, watching them move beneath the silky blouse as she danced.

She twirled, and he saw her face. She was smiling. She sang, and she danced to her singing, and she was good. It was her smile that held him and broke through his discomfort. He began to smile back, and she began to do to Jimmy Dela what Astaire had done and Kelly and all those smiling dancers in all those films had done. She took him away somewhere where there were no signals or sirens, and everyone was free to be foolish.

She sang and hummed and mugged and made up steps and combinations, laughing out loud sometimes. He laughed, too. The taps rattled on the kitchen floor, blackening the linoleum. The people downstairs knocked on the ceiling. Dela knocked back. The phone rang and Ellen danced toward it.

"Wait."

The tone of his voice stopped her, chilled her. He was staring at the phone, and he had changed, had become tight and serious again. He was listening for the ring pattern that Sergeant Raye used. This wasn't it. The phone just kept ringing.

"It's the people downstairs, I bet." Ellen stared at him. "Don't you think?"

"Answer it."

He stood up and came toward her as she picked up the phone.

"Hello?"

"Ellen?"

"Yes."

"Ellen Skate?"

She held her breath. He was there—in that silence at the other end of the phone. That was *his* silence. She was sure. She rushed to hang up before something could come through those wires and touch her. She slammed the receiver down and stared at Dela. He wasn't looking at her. He was thinking, leaning against the wall.

"That was *him*," she said.

"What did he say?"

"Just . . . Ellen Skate."

"Could've been anybody." He walked away from her.

"He knows I'm here!"

He walked into Ann's dark bedroom. "Could've been anybody."

"Anybody would call back, wouldn't they?" She followed him. "Wouldn't they? If I had hung up on somebody else, they'd just call back." She waited. Dela stood back from the window, staring at the drapes, thinking. It was very quiet. "If it was someone else, the phone'd be ringing right now. Anyway, I know it's him. I felt it."

"What did he sound like?"

She thought, shrugged. "Regular. Just . . . young. Younger than I thought. I thought he'd have the voice of an old man."

"His voice *is* old." Dela still didn't turn to her. "I talked to him on the phone."

"When?"

"In Chicago. Months ago. It's an old voice. This wasn't him."

"You never talked to him."

He moved to the window, but didn't touch the drape. "I staked out his hotel room. Almost caught him, but he knew. He called."

"What did he say?"

"He said, 'I'm coming . . . but you won't see me.' And he did. And I didn't see him."

She moved through the silence, went to him. "He came underground. He can do that. And through walls." Now Dela turned to her. She went on. "He can be a bird, a snake. He's an avenging spirit, and if he knows where I am, he'll get me. Nobody can stop him. That's why I can't wait for him. I have to move on."

He looked at her a moment, then he turned back to the window, pulling the drape away from the glass. Now, Nye, he thought, look up here. See her. Make sure. Come for her. Now. "Ellen," he said, "I want you to look out there."

"He'll see me."

"He isn't out there. Go ahead."

She stepped slowly to the glass and looked out over the buildings, looked down into the street. She moved her head slowly from side to side, searching. She saw nothing in the light of the street lamps, no one at the lighted windows across the way, but she felt him there in the shadows, deep in the blackest shadows, watching her. She drew in a quick breath and turned to Dela, stared at him, her eyes widening with a new thought. She whispered. "You want him to see me." She stepped back from the window, and he let the drape fall back in place. "You know he's out there." Dela shook his head, but she went on, "You *want* him to come."

"He's not there."

"You don't care if he kills me, as long as you catch him."

"No. I want to stop him, to *stop* him from killing you. I couldn't stop him before. This time I will. I promise."

"I don't want to be here."

"He's not out there!" Dela quieted, took a breath. "He's not."

"You sure?"

He nodded, certain that Nye was close, hoping that he had seen her.

She studied him. "You care what happens to Kathleen Orista?"

He nodded.

"And you didn't stand me at that window for him to see?"

He shook his head. "I want to keep you alive."

"Why?"

That stopped him a moment.

"Say the right thing, Dela. Why?"

He shrugged. "I like you."

"That was it." She smiled, her eyes still wondering, watching him. "You're Kathleen's first friend."

In a moment he put out his hand. "Glad to meet you." She shook the hand, grinning. Then he said, "Go to bed now, okay?"

"It's early."

"Go to bed."

"Dela . . ."

"What?"

"You said that until Nye gets caught, you and me are just inches away."

"Don't worry about it."

"Where are you sleeping tonight?"

"Don't worry about it. I'm an officer of the law. You're safe."

"You say that now."

"Go to bed."

"What about in the middle of the night when you wake up trembling with lust and come into my room with your badge off?"

"Go to bed."

"Give me your gun for under my pillow."

"Are you going to bed?"

"There's no lock on my door."

"Goddamn it . . ."

"Don't touch me."

He picked her up in his arms.

"Oh my God, somebody help."

He smiled in spite of himself, carrying her out of the room, shaking his head. "Jesus."

"Police!"

"Shut up, will you? For Christ's sake?"

He carried her into her own room.

"Where's a cop when you need one?"

He dropped her on the bed. "Now sleep!"

She bounced on the bed, smiling at him, making him smile. In that instant, with the bed still shaking beneath her and Dela grinning above her, a little laugh, like a piccolo, like a child's laugh, trickled from her throat. She was playing with a friend. They were rolling in the grass.

He turned to leave.

"Wait."

He glanced back at her. She raised a foot off the bed, raised a shoe for him to take off. He made a face, came to her, pulled the tap shoe off and tossed it over his shoulder. It clattered somewhere. She laughed and raised the other. He took it off. "Now sleep. I'll see you in the morning."

She nodded. They looked at each other a moment. He left.

There was no way Nye could get to any of the windows, except the window beside the door. That door and window faced the second-floor balcony. Dela sat on the floor, in the dark, and watched that door. Before him on the rug was his revolver, his detective shield, and Ellen's tap shoe. He had carried the shoe with him absently as he left her room nearly an hour ago. He had listened to her stirring on the bed, getting comfortable, maybe getting under the covers, maybe undressed. She had been quiet for a long time.

Part of what he had told her had been true. He *did*

care. He *did* want to keep her alive—not only because she was Nye's target, but because she was somebody he liked. He would like Ellen Skate for a friend, or Kathleen Orista, or whoever the musketeer was. He enjoyed her energy and humor, all of it jumping out of her eyes. He liked the way she looked, too. Her body would feel good against him, would fit just right against him, her small, smooth body.

Nye wanted that body, too. He wanted to tear out that energy, empty those eyes, leave her cold and stiff and still. Dela wouldn't let him.

I'll kill you, fucker. Dela lay on his stomach, touched the handle of the revolver in front of him. Old crazy asshole. Come and try it. Come now. Dela gripped the revolver and picked it up off the floor, pointed it at the door, aimed it chest high. He held it there until his hand shook and sweat broke on his forehead. Bastard, look what you've got me doing. He lowered his arm to the floor, and rested his head on it. Nye had him pretending, playing guns. He had him secretly holding an intended victim. He had him doing lousy police work. He had him standing that girl at the window.

He got to his feet and walked to the door, double locked it, checked the locks on the window. He pocketed his shield, holstered the gun, and walked into Ellen's room.

He moved softly to the side of the bed. He put his hands on his hips and stared at her. She was turned away from him, just her head showing above the covers. Her clothes were on the floor. He watched her a while. Then he reached out to put a hand on her shoulder, but she spoke, wide awake.

"That is you, isn't it?"

He whispered. "Yeah."

She turned over on her back. He could barely make out her face, her smile. "I knew I couldn't trust you."

"Listen to me." He stared the smile off her face. He kept whispering, though there was no need. "I'm calling the police. They'll run you home. Then you and your parents are leaving for a while. Mexico, I think."

She stared a long time. "Why?"

"That's the way to do it. With you safe, out of the way. We comb this place. We set traps. We get the bastard. With you safe."

But he hadn't answered her. "Why, Dela?"

He sighed. He sat on the bed. "I put you at that window. I set you up. I wanted him—but not like a policeman. You know what I mean? I let him turn me into something else. No more."

She kept staring. Her eyes were shiny with tears now. "You changed your mind."

"Yeah."

"Why?"

He shrugged. He met her stare. "It wasn't right. It wasn't good for *you*."

The tears were in her whisper. "You care about Kathleen Orista?"

He nodded. "She's a friend of mine."

They stared. She blinked, and a tear moved down her cheek. He rose from the bed.

"Dela."

"Yeah?"

"Don't call now."

He stopped.

"Sit down again, okay?"

He sat on the bed. She drew an arm out of the covers to place over her eyes for a moment. "Call in the morning, all right?" When she lowered her arm, the tears were gone. "All right?"

He didn't answer.

"Dela . . . I'd rather spend the night with a friend. Okay?"

In a moment he nodded.

"Could you just . . . sit there a minute?" He nodded again, and he reached for her hand, held it. She closed her eyes. In a while, she turned on her side, away from him, and he let go of her hand.

He sat beside her, and he wanted very much to hold her. He whispered, "I'm . . . sorry," and he thought she nodded. He sat for a long, silent moment, and then he said, "I'd like to hold you."

She didn't move. When she spoke, the tears were back in her voice. "Will you sleep with me all night?"

"Yes."

He took off his clothes and got under the covers, not touching her yet. Then he put a hand on her back and slid it to her shoulder, held it there a while.

She turned to him.

He could see her open eyes, searching his, and he understood. They must look at each other. They could not close their eyes and be just two bodies. Her eyes said, "I'm me," and at the same time they questioned him. His eyes answered, "I know. I know you. And I'm me."

They stared, and they smiled shyly, like new friends, and they began.

Dela was strong, and he used his strength to make

himself gentle. He used his boxer's muscles to hold his weight off her, touching her without crushing her.

She used her swift, dancer's body to make her movements slow, to turn and touch and pause with easy grace.

They each made a sound like crying as he entered her, a sound full of pleasure and wonder and love.

Nye watched the window. He sat on the floor in the back seat of his car, in darkness, out of sight. He could see the window where the girl had stood, the same girl who had paused at the mailbox, the girl who said yes on the telephone when he asked, "Ellen?" She was the last of the five. Or she was a trap. He would wait and watch the window. He had time. He had only one thing to do in his life.

Ellen? Are you in there? Are you alone? Are you in bed? Asleep? We want to be with you. You've never been with anyone like us. We want to hold you. We'll give you what no one has ever given you. We'll take you where you've never been. Come with us, Ellen. We're waiting. We're watching the window. Come with Randy and me.

17

ELLEN woke up in darkness, her head under the covers. It could have been any time of night or day, any place at all. She could have been twelve years old or four. At times like this, still connected to sleep by long sweet strands of honey, she felt she could pick her place and time. She could choose to wake up anywhere in her life. She searched for a happy time. She remembered Dela and smiled and pushed the covers off her face.

Daylight was tracing the edges of the drapes. She heard Dela making those soft kitchen sounds, those morning clinks and clatters that start the day smelling of coffee. She rolled on her back and spread wide on the bed, her small fists, her feet turning and twisting, stretching every muscle. Then she relaxed and moved her legs slowly under the sheet, feeling the warm places and the cool places, remembering.

He had trembled in her arms. They had both been shaken by the power and pleasure of it, and they had trembled together. They had held each other afterward, all the way to sleep.

She slid out of bed and went to the mirror. She wanted to see the body he had held last night. She studied it and was surprised by her rush of pride. She stared with wonder at those places where his hands had gone, those parts of herself touched by his arms and legs and his lips. She remembered the shapes and textures of his body, and she wanted to be there again, with him again.

She saw him in the mirror. He came suddenly to the doorway and then stopped and moved back into the hall. "Sorry," he said.

She stared at the doorway a moment. He was waiting out of sight. "It's all right." But he didn't come in, and his silence made her embarrassed, made her go to her slacks and blouse and hurry into them.

"I made coffee," he said from the hall.

She went to the doorway. He was fully dressed. He had even shaved. He didn't smile, and his distance chilled her. "Have you called yet?"

He shook his head. "I wanted you to be awake."

She nodded. He started to turn back to the kitchen. "Just a minute. All right? Dela?" He stopped and stared at her. She waited a moment. "Don't you remember?" His look softened, but he didn't speak. "Will you hold me a minute?" She stepped up against him and put her arms around him, closed her eyes. In a moment she felt his arms encircle her and press her to him. "You remember?"

He whispered into her hair. "Yes."

"Then what's wrong?" She pulled back to look at him. "Dela, you're not smiling."

"I have to make the phone call. You have to go to Mexico."

"Not necessarily."

He sighed and half grinned at her, shook his head at her spirit. She wouldn't quit. "Have some coffee." He started to turn away, but she held on.

"Wait. Just listen. Listen! Okay? Wait." He stood there. "Think of this. Ready? What if we both went to Chicago? Right now." Her eyes grew wider, watching him. He only sighed. "Now wait. Think! You call the cops and say, 'Forget it. I'm going home to Chicago. You guys catch him.' I write my parents and say, 'Goodbye. I'm traveling the world.' We both go to Chicago. Right now! Dela! I won't bother you. I'll find a place. I'll find a job, but there we'll both be—in Chicago!"

Before he had seemed only distant, nervous. Now he looked sad, looked away from her.

"Think about it."

"I said I was going back to being a good policeman. I wasn't going to let him change me into . . ."

"Be a good cop in Chicago!"

"I couldn't leave this case."

"Yes you could! You could go home to Chicago, and I could go too. I can go anywhere in the world, but I pick Chicago. That's a sacrifice, Dela. If I can give up the Caribbean for you, you can give up one lousy murder case for me!"

"I can't."

"Why!? Why can't we just go!?"

He waited a moment, then he said, "He'd still be out there."

She nodded, growing quiet. "All right. Okay. But death is *always* out there, isn't it? That doesn't stop people."

"It's Nye. I want him."

"More than you want *me*? Jesus Christ, Dela." Tears broke in her voice now. "I'm willing to go to cold, crummy Chicago for you and work in a junky night club or a little hole of a drafty theater while I go to dance classes every goddamn day just so you and I can have weekends and afternoons together once in a while and go to the Fuckingham Fountain and walk down goddamn Michigan Avenue, and you tell me you prefer the company of this crazy old murdering *man*!"

She was angry at herself for starting to cry. He put his hands on her shoulders and imagined her there in Chicago, inside his life, inside his apartment, the lights already on when he came home from work and all her energy waiting for him, her eyes and her smile, her smooth, taut young body. He could hear their voices shredding the calm and quiet of his place with shouts and laughter. He held her very close and closed his eyes, seeing how it could be with her and listening to their voices. But the sirens came and drowned them out. The warning signals came and cautioned him—don't be a fool.

"Dela."

He slid his hands from her, moved away from her.

"Aw, Dela." She leaned a shoulder against the hallway wall, watching him walk into the kitchen. "Shit." She listened. He was pouring coffee. "You're going to call, aren't you?"

"Yes."

"Shit." She rubbed at the tears with the palms of her hands. "Well, wait. Can you wait while I take a shower? Can I have half a goddamn hour?" She waited a moment.

"Yes."

"Thank you." She stepped into the bathroom and started the water. "Dela!"

He shouted back over the sound of the water. "What?"

"I want to hear you. I want to know you're out there, so talk to me."

"You want coffee?"

"No! Talk to me." She stood in the hall, thinking a moment. Then she closed the bathroom door and went quickly and quietly into the living room. He didn't see her pass the kitchen. He was still sending his voice into the bathroom. "I'll call and have them come here in half an hour."

She picked up her purse and boots and went to the front door. She heard him dialing the phone. She unlocked the door and went out, closed it softly behind her, and walked quickly down the stairs to the street.

As he bit into an apple and glanced up from the history book he was pretending to read, Nye saw her—the girl from yesterday, the girl from the window. He had stayed awake for this, with his body cold and aching and the daylight burning his eyes. He had hoped for this and imagined it, and now it was happening. She was there, barefoot and carrying her boots, hurrying down the street.

He climbed into the front seat of the camper, keeping his movements careful and sure. He reached for the key and started the engine, glancing into his mirror to find her. She was turning to face the oncoming cars. She was hitchhiking.

He pulled directly across the street into a driveway, then backed up. He had to stop and wait for two cars. Then he roared backward into the street and headed toward her. He braked. One of the cars had stopped for her. She was getting in. The car pulled away and he followed it, steadying himself. His chest was tight, shuddering with cold and with anticipation.

He stared at the car ahead and through the back window to the girl's dark tangled hair and through her hair and her skull to her mind. Ellen? Ellen Skate? It's us.

"Listen, *you* come and pick her up. Because I know you. Bring a wig. . . . Yes. If he's out there watching the place, I want him to think she's still in here. . . . Then bring a hat or something, a coat that'll fit her. Jesus. A beard and sunglasses. . . . Yeah. . . . Same to you." Dela hung up. He sipped his coffee and then ambled toward the bathroom. "Okay, thirty minutes." He stood at the door, leaned on it. "They're taking you to the airport. You'll meet your parents there. I guess they'll . . . bring your clothes." He sipped again. There was no sound from her, only the water roaring and tumbling. She must have it on full. "I'm not sure it's Mexico. Could be anywhere." He paused a moment. She said nothing. "Could even be Chicago." When she didn't respond to that, he hit the doorknob fast and stepped in, angry at her for sulking, for making him feel he had let her down, for making him want to grab her and hold her and tell her he remembered every minute of it, and he wanted her again right now, and he wanted her sitting on the floor of his apartment having a glass of the wine he had saved and laughing with her eyes and moving to his music.

The empty room stopped him, scared him. He went quickly into her bedroom. "Ellen!" He ran into the living room and saw that her purse was gone, and her boots. "Jesus." The word was tortured in his throat. "Christ." Then he was down the stairs and out on the street in the two-way river of students, his eyes bouncing from one to the next. "Ellen!" His voice stopped that river, turned the faces to him. His shout was so full of fear and regret. "Kathleen!"

There was a young couple in the front seat. Ellen was in back, putting on her boots.

"We're going to Culver City. How about you?"

"Fine."

"Fine?"

"Culver City'll be fine."

The man giggled, and the woman turned around to look at her. "You don't care where you're going?"

Ellen leaned back, sighed, glad to be in motion. She tried not to think of Dela, of the shower water still running, of last night. "Sure I care."

"Well? Where you heading?"

"Culver City."

The couple smiled at each other, and the woman shrugged. They drove a while. Then she turned to Ellen again. "What'll you do in Culver City?"

Ellen shrugged. "I'll decide where to go next. Maybe the Caribbean. You don't need a passport for Jamaica, right?"

The man giggled again. "You can't hitchhike to Jamaica."

"Argentina, then. Someplace warm."

"Nice to be that free," the woman said.

"Maybe Rio . . . I don't know. Mexico City. No. That's too close. I don't know. I'll pick someplace. I'll make a list."

They let her off on Culver Boulevard and waved, and she turned to the traffic and put out her thumb, nervous about being stopped, anxious to be on her way anywhere. There was a high wailing of loose old brakes and she was faced with a scratched and faded painting of a sunset. The door of the camper was swung open for her, leaving a hole in the painted sky. She got in.

"Hi."

The man smiled at her, but didn't speak. He pulled into traffic. It was an old, comfortable camper. Ellen stretched her legs in front of her, leaned back on the seat, and looked out of her window. "Don't ask," she said. "I haven't decided yet. Just go where you're going and drop me off." She watched people a while, and store windows, saw a police car and thought of Dela and what he might be doing, where in the apartment he might be standing. She pictured him at the window, watching for her. "Do you happen to have a pen and paper? I need to make a list. Or better yet, a world map and a dart."

The man chuckled and she turned to him. He glanced at her as he drove, his eyes crinkled and even watery with humor. He had a big, overgrown mustache, a seaman's knit cap, and a lovingly crushed and battered leather jacket. He seemed as worn and comfortable as his musty, dusty camper. He was about forty-five, she guessed, or maybe older. "Map and a dart." He laughed and shook his head. "Hey, I got a pen and a notebook in back."

She turned to her window again. "That's okay, I get sick if I try to write in a car."

"Chyken."

"What?"

He was still smiling, shaking his head, recalling something. "That's what we called it for short. 'Chyken.' A hitchhiker was a chyker . . . for short, y' know? I hitchhiked. I chyked one long trip. From school in Illinois to Fort Lauderdale. Told my parents I had a ride so they wouldn't worry. Then . . . about a month after I was back, I told my father. I was proud. 'Dad, Bob and I chyked it—all the way.'"

"What did he say?"

The man still shook his head, but he lost his smile. "I said. . . . Whew, I turned white, I guess. I felt sick. I thought of him on the road. 'Think what could've happened,' I said. I made him promise he'd never try it again."

She watched him, confused. "Who?"

He turned to her, his smile on again. "Rand. My name's Rand."

"I'm Kathleen Orista."

He chuckled, his head shaking and his eyes watering at the humor of it all. He glanced from her to the road and back.

She smiled, watching him. "You don't like it?"

"That's not your name."

"It is if I say it is."

"Naah."

"You don't think it suits me?"

"Nope."

"What do I look like? How about . . . Helena Traveste?"

He laughed loudly and kept laughing, wiping his eyes as he drove. He had her laughing too.

"All right, what? What suits me? You pick one."

He thought a moment, still grinning, wiping his eyes with the back of a hand. He pulled into an alley and stopped, sat back from the wheel. He turned to her and laughed, and she laughed too. Then he said, "Ellen."

Her expression froze and then began to melt, sliding from happiness into surprise, from wonder to realization. Him. Nye. That was him behind the beard, inside those old eyes, reaching for her now with old, wrinkled hands, long fingers, the claws of a Fury. She screamed a low, mindless scream, wrenching around to throw herself at the door.

She felt his claws in her hair. She felt his power pulling her back and then swinging her hard. The metal dashboard rushed toward her and she closed her eyes, felt the impact on her forehead.

There was no pain at first. She was limp and he was moving her, putting cloth in her mouth, something tight on her wrists.

She was huddled and twisted on the floor of the front seat when the pain in her head began drumming her back to full consciousness. Her hands were tied behind her, and her ankles were bound. She was gagged.

She turned her head to look at him. From her angle he was giantlike—his long legs, his large hands on the wheel, his head nearly touching the roof. He was watching the road, driving fast, and he was crying slightly, silently.

Nye had pictured Randy at eighteen, hitchhiking to Florida. He imagined how the boy must have looked to a driver. He passed Randy again and again, a tall handsome boy on the roadside with a duffle bag, a sign—"Ft. Lauderd'l," a smile, the wind in his light hair. He stopped and let one of these visions into his car. "School vacation?" "Yes sir." "Parents don't mind that you hitchhike?" "Well, they worry. My dad . . . I'm writing him postcards as if I'm in a car, y' know? He thinks about me all the time . . . what I'm doing. He calls me at school a lot. We have nice long talks—about everything. My dad and I are really close. Very, very close."

Nye turned to smile at the boy, but Randy was sixteen years old and pleading, "Can I try it now?" "Wait, wait, Rand. Watch me a while more. Watch my feet. Clutch in. Now look. I shift. Clutch out slowly." "I know, Dad." "You don't know. You see, but you don't *know*. Not yet. Takes time." "Let me try it." "I will. Do you know the signals?" "Yes." "Watch when I turn. I let up on the gas, turning now. Clutch in to downshift. Up slowly on the clutch. See?" "Yeah, Dad. I can do it." "It's timing, Rand. It's like rubbing your

stomach and patting your head at the same time."
"Dad? Look."

Nye turned to see his son smiling at him, proudly rubbing small circles on his belly, patting the knit cap on his head. Nye began to cry slightly, silently. The road in front of him blurred, and he wiped his eyes with his fingers, wiped away Randy at sixteen, at eighteen. He remembered who he was with and where he was going. He looked at her tied and twisted on the floor of the passenger side. She just fit. She could barely move. She was watching him.

"Your forehead is red and swollen. Does it hurt?" She didn't move, kept her eyes on him. "What are you thinking? What's going through your mind right now? Hm? Are you praying? Confessing? Saying goodbye? The last thoughts of Ellen Skate. The deathbed ramblings—with no one to hear, no one with a microphone to catch the last whisper. Tell Harry I love him. Give my cat to Alice. I regret I have but one life . . . 'Tis a far, far better thing . . . Rosebud. I'm dying, Egypt. There's no place like home."

He glanced at her. She had turned away from him, leaned her head against the camper wall, near the door. He spoke louder, watching the road again.

"It doesn't matter what you're thinking. You may as well leave it blank. Count from one to a thousand. It'll be over then. Are you wondering how? Does it matter? Nothing about you matters. I need you to close the circle, that's all. That's your only purpose. Have you ever wondered about that? Have you searched for the meaning of your life? Most people do. They go around starving for goals and missions and callings. Did you think you'd find it in religion? Or in marriage? Motherhood? Medicine? Or in doing some great service for the retarded or the mute or the natives of Brazil? Well . . . I give you your calling. It was waiting. That's all it ever was—waiting for me. I am the purpose of your life. This trip we're taking is what your whole life has built toward. You've been waiting to die by my hands, to close the circle of events your father began twenty years ago." He shrugged. "Now you know. Most people never find any purpose for their lives. But you discovered yours. Feel better?"

As he spoke to her, Ellen moved by millimeters, slid her face closer and closer to the window crank on the door. She listened. She heard him tell her she had no purpose in life but death, but most of her mind was focused on that little metal knob. The plastic had been broken off. The metal piece could fit under her gag, lift it off. The cloth in her mouth could be moved by her tongue. She could spit it out. When he stopped at a traffic light, she could pull the gag off and free her mouth and scream. She moved slowly. She felt the chill of metal on her cheek.

"What are you thinking? Are you thinking about what you're going to do? Are you thinking about tomorrow? People do that. People think they go around with a past, present, and future. The future is myth. They think it's solid because it appears on calendars, because they write reminders to themselves and make lists, make dates. It's all myth. I can wipe it away. I do. I hereby cancel your future. I can do that. The others had plans and datebooks. Dreams. Visions of themselves in cities they had never seen. They'll never see those cities. I wiped it all away. Have you ever been to Rome? No? Then for you there will never be Rome. For you it will never again be morning. Your plans are just so much smoke."

She screamed.

He turned to her with a look of terror and concern, wondering why, why was she screaming? What was wrong? Then he realized she was screaming for her life, screaming to be heard. He raced the engine to cover her scream. She stopped to draw in a breath and he let up on the gas. Then he raced it again as she screamed. They were stopped at a red light. There was no other traffic, no one on the corners, only a child on a skateboard halfway down the block. No one heard. He sat back from the wheel, watching her, racing the engine as her last scream changed to sobbing. She struck the door with her head and tried to kick with her bound boots. The light changed, and he eased the camper ahead, glancing at her as she sobbed great hiccuping sobs and twisted and kicked.

"It's like I've been to market, Ellen. I've got this trussed-up turkey or chicken or rabbit in my car . . . and the thing knows, senses it's going to be killed. It's down there kicking on the floor of my . . ."

"*Goddamn you!*" She shouted through her sobbing, turning her tear-washed face at him, the gag down around her neck. "I'm a person! I'm not a fucking chicken!"

His voice was calm. He watched the road. "You're the last piece in the circle. You have no place to go and nothing to do except to act out your part in our play. That's where you fit in. That's your place in the world."

"I have better things to do! Better! I don't give a shit about your goddamn *circles!*"

"You think Randy and I came into your life by chance? It was set in motion twenty years ago. You sensed it, didn't you? Where were you going? Nowhere. Talking about a map and a dart. You were waiting for us."

"No." Her sobbing had quieted. She pressed her face into her raised knees, kept it there a while. Then she looked at him again. "No, I've decided where I'm going. This is very definite. Hey! I've made up my mind! Listen! I'm going to Chicago." Her voice broke, and her face dipped down to her knees again.

"You're going to the forest, and that's the last place in the world you'll go."

She bit into the bunched material of her slacks, clenched her teeth and screamed inside her mind. She knew what would happen to her now. The metal bands that hurt her wrists were handcuffs. He was taking her to the forest. It would be fire.

The map had told him, Angeles Crest National Forest, but it wasn't what he had expected. He was driving high into the Angeles Mountains, mountains of low shrubs and bare earth. He went up thousands of feet and felt the air turn cold. He spotted evergreens on a ridge off the road, and he pulled into a turn-off opposite the mountain side of the highway, drove to its edge. He was looking down into a gorge, a small canyon with a trail that could take him deeper into vegetation. An occasional car or truck passed on the highway. There was no sign of life below in the gorge. He turned off the engine. "We're here."

She spoke without looking at him. Her voice was soft. "Just untie me and . . . open the door. I'll walk away. My parents . . . everybody will think you killed me. They'll never see me again. I promise. I'll go to my friend in Chicago. Ellen Skate will be dead. That's all you want. My father will think you killed me. That's what you want. You don't really need to kill me. I'll just disappear. I promise you. Ellen Skate will be dead. I'll be Kathleen Orista. Okay?"

She heard the jingle of keys. He moved close to her and turned her, unlocked the cuffs and took them off. She was afraid to look at him. She thought he might be doing what she asked, and she wouldn't spoil it by looking at him or speaking. She barely breathed. He clicked open a pocket knife and sawed at the rope on her boots, freed her legs.

"Sit up here with me."

Her legs were stiff and couldn't support her. He pulled her up to sit on the seat next to him. He put an arm around her and brought her head against his shoulder. They remained that way a while. Then he spoke softly. "Randy is here. Now. In this camper. He's holding you. That's his touch you feel. And he feels you against him. He likes holding you this way. He's able to enjoy it—this dead boy—because his spirit is coming alive inside of me, more and more. I can give some bits of life to him, some sensations. He smells your hair right now. He . . . feels how soft your cheek is, the warmth of it. He wants to kiss you. He does. I'll put his mouth on yours, Ellen, and he'll feel it. Here. Turn." He kissed trembling lips, tasted tears. "He can feel that . . . because of what I've been doing these past months. That's why he's stirring inside of me. I have to *keep* doing it. I have to finish it."

"No . . ."

"Shh. Yes. I do. I do."

"Please . . ."

"I have to. I do. Now just . . . slide along the seat. We're getting out on my side. Don't try to yell or fight. There's no way you can change any of this. You can't affect it in any way. Believe me. It's like trying to stop nightfall or the rain. Just come with us to the forest, and we'll finish it now." His hand was already opening the door on his side, and he was moving, sliding her with him, trapping her against him with his other hand.

She waited until he was half out the door and she was behind the wheel, and she broke free of him and hit the horn. He had the keys, and there was no sound. She grabbed the wheel and wouldn't let go. He pulled at her fingers, peeling them off the plastic, bending them until she cried out. She pushed at him and lunged out of the camper. He caught her arm, and she pulled away, running and stumbling. He caught her shoulders from behind and pulled back the cloth of her blouse, popping the buttons, pulling the material off her and down her arms to the buttoned cuffs where it caught.

She fell, and he brought her up on her feet, using the blouse like a rope between them. He moved quickly down the hill, pulling her after him. He kept glancing back until they were out of sight of the highway.

She tried to twist free, tried to turn and kick him. He yanked her hard and she fell. He pulled her up again, and the blouse came loose from her wrists. She ran, pushing through bushes that scratched her arms and her bare stomach and breasts. She stumbled over rocks and fell on hands that were bleeding but felt no pain. All the while he was behind her, a presence with outstretched claws, a sound of panting and trampling, a large, hulking, branch-breaking thing just inches from her back.

He caught her by pushing her. She fell, and he fell on top of her, his heavy body trapping her, pinning her legs, his hands catching hers and forcing them to the ground. Both of them were out of breath, and he lay on top of her a while.

In a moment, he half rose. He sat across her middle, letting her hands free. She laid the backs of them over her face, tears coming. Small liquid sobs whimpered from her throat. These were the only sounds now. The leaves raised by the chase had settled back to the earth. The scattered birds and mice and lizards were still again, listening perhaps to the sobbing of the girl on the ground.

Nye watched her a moment. He looked at her breasts and then touched them softly as she cried. He brushed dirt and leaves from her chest and arms, picked them from her hair. She took her hands from her face, staring at him. He moved her hair back and touched her bruised forehead, traced around the scratches on her cheeks.

She spoke through her sobbing. "Do you want me?" She touched his hand. He loomed above her, slowly shaking his head no, but his look was deep and soft, his voice a whisper.

"We have to finish it."

"Randy? Do you want me?"

He put his fingertips to her nipples, gently circled her soft flesh as it shook with her crying.

"Randy. Please?"

"We have to finish it now."

"Randy, don't hurt me."

Nye looked at her, then he rose and stood above her. He put a hand down to help her rise.

"Let Randy love me."

He took her hand, and she pulled it away. "Please! He wants to. He wouldn't hurt me. I *know* it. I know *him*."

He stood her up roughly, held her arms.

"I *know* Randy. I know why he wanted to be kidnapped that night."

He walked her forward toward the trees. "*Wanted* to be!"

"Yes! *Glad* to be. Happy to be part of it. Not watching it for once, but *part* of it, in the center of it. I know about that. I know him! I like him. Wait! I like Randy. He wouldn't hurt me. He wouldn't!"

He sat her down by a tree.

"Don't! Wait!"

He pulled her arms back around the trunk and took the handcuffs from his pocket. One of his hands held both her wrists, his fingers tying them together like long hard ropes. Then the cuffs were on and clicked.

"God . . . *damn* it!" She kicked and pulled and rose up almost to her knees, but a low branch held her down. "Wait!" He was moving about, gathering dry wood, breaking long branches over his knee, raking dry leaves with his hands, raking them toward her. "Wait! I never hurt him! I didn't do anything! My father didn't mean it! Nye! *Randy*! I have to be someplace. I have to be in Chicago!" She closed her eyes, crying and speaking mostly to herself now, shivering with icy fear. "Really. I'm going to dance in Chicago. I really. . . . Jesus! Oh God. . . . Dela! Dela, look, I'm here. Guess who. I said I'd come. Can I come in? Dela, I like your place. Yes. Okay. I'll stay, Dela. Dela. Dela! Mama! Daddy! Nye, I'm not my father! I'm not! *I'm not my father! I'm me!*"

He spread his pile of dry leaves toward the twigs and brittle branches that surrounded the girl. He was ready. It was almost over. He pulled out a book of matches and trembled and laughed at how much he was trembling, at how excited they were, he and Randy. Oh God, Rand. Didn't I say I'd do it? Didn't I do it? God. Look. That's the last one—that girl. And this is the match. This is how it began. Now. I end it.

He touched the match to the leaves. They burned, but slowly. He lit more matches and threw them on the pile. It was a fire now. It crackled. It warmed him. He stood and moved back. Ellen was murmuring, shivering, the fire's heat made her open her eyes. She saw the flames, and she screamed with her mouth closed and her face turned away. She screamed again.

Nye stepped back again as the fire became a blaze. He slowly raised his hands, thrust his arms out stiff in front of him. The circle of the universe was closing tight. She screamed aloud. He could barely see her through the flames and smoke. The universe was moving. The giant tumblers of mammoth locks were falling into place with clicks like thunder. He pushed his hands toward the fire until his shoulders ached.

She screamed a different scream, and the sound slashed at him. This was a new sound, a mad sound, without hope. It had death in it. He listened to it and felt his throat fill with tears. The scream came again, like a sharp blade lunging out of the fire and into his chest. He cried out in pain. The scream wasn't Ellen's. She had disappeared into air thick and rippling with heat. This sound came from another throat. Randy was screaming, screaming at him from beyond the flames.

"Please!" A shrill, mindless scream that was no longer a word. "EEE!"

Nye's breath was caught, his eyes wide with disbelief. "Randy!" A sob shook him loose, and he was suddenly moving, thrusting his hands toward the fire. "Randy!" In one hand he held, between finger and thumb, the key to the handcuffs.

"EEEE!"

He pushed that hand ahead of him, through the flames, through the waves of heat, through the screams. He pushed that key toward the tiny lock on the handcuffs, reaching forward until his right arm was impossibly long and stretching longer, disconnecting at the shoulder, leaping cartoonlike to carry the key into that small invisible hole and turn. Turn. It did turn, and the cuffs fell away from the bloody wrists, and Stephen Nye took his son into his arms and lifted him and ran, ran out of the flames to the cool, still forest.

He fell on his knees, still cradling his boy, then he eased him to the ground and stared at him.

It was Ellen, Ellen Skate, a stranger. She looked at him with wild eyes and moved away, crawled and slid away, watching him, glancing at the fire that followed them. It was Ellen. It was not his son.

He sat limply on the ground, his hands loose and

empty in his lap. His son was dead. She was a stranger. All of them had been strangers—the fathers, the sons and wives and daughters. None of them had mattered. His son was dead, and Stephen Nye had not been given a chance to do what he should have done, what he would have done, what fathers forever have whispered in secret prayer: Please, my life for his. Stephen Nye had not been allowed to trade his life for his son's in that fiery moment twenty years ago.

He watched the girl stand and turn and run. He heard the flames rushing behind him, great billows of fire like eager arms reaching and snatching at everything alive, turning life into smoke. He waited.